This whole day ... ... was *before* a gia... tree.

"I didn't expect to b... ...nodded at the dog, whose eyes hadn't left Matt for a second. "Is it safe for me to come down?"

"Sure. As long as you leave once you do. This is private property."

One thing at a time. Matt slid toward the spot where the trunk split, then jumped to the ground. She flinched when he did—his first clue that she might be as frightened as she was angry. He stayed close to the tree, avoiding making direct eye contact with the dog, who was giving out a low growl at regular intervals. He worked at keeping his voice as calm as possible.

"I'm sorry I alarmed you, but I'm actually the new owner of this property. And you are...?"

She stepped back. "You are *not*. This is *my* land. And the only other private property near here is the ski lodge, and it's in foreclosure."

"I know. I just bought it."

Her mouth dropped open. "You...you *couldn't* have..."

* * *

GALLANT LAKE STORIES: At home on the water!

Dear Reader,

I'm thrilled to be telling more stories from the fictional town of Gallant Lake in the Catskill Mountains of New York. Gallant Lake is a small resort town trying to make a comeback after some hard years—one romance at a time. That *rebuilding* theme truly resonates in these pandemic times and makes me love this award-winning series all the more.

In *Her Mountainside Haven*, Jillie Coleman is a woman with serious anxiety issues, including agoraphobia. That disorder is associated with people who never leave their homes, often because they're terrified of having a panic attack in public. Jillie has created many work-arounds in her life to deal with her anxiety issues. And it works just fine for her, until Matt Danzer arrives in Gallant Lake to reopen the old ski lodge next door, disrupting her quiet life. Jillie doesn't have any work-around for falling in love.

Matt has no plans to stay. He made a graveside vow to his parents to care for his globe-trotting younger brother, even if Bryce tells him it's not necessary. Matt and Jillie will both have to make some big changes for their love to work.

I have anxiety issues myself. While love alone cannot "cure" an anxiety disorder, it can be the motivation needed to seek professional help. If anxiety is affecting your life, please reach out to someone, like I did. There are resources available to help, and they can change your life.

Happy reading,

Jo McNally

Her Mountainside Haven

JO McNALLY

———

HARLEQUIN

SPECIAL
EDITION

HARLEQUIN®
SPECIAL EDITION™

Recycling programs
for this product may
not exist in your area.

ISBN-13: 978-1-335-40469-5

Her Mountainside Haven

Harlequin Enterprises ULC
22 Adelaide St. West, 40th Floor
Toronto, Ontario M5H 4E3, Canada
www.Harlequin.com

Printed in U.S.A.

Jo McNally lives in upstate New York with one hundred pounds of dog and two hundred pounds of husband—her slice of the bed is very small. When she's not writing or reading romance novels (or clinging to the edge of the bed), she can often be found on the back porch sipping wine with friends while listening to great music. If the weather is absolutely perfect, Jo might join her husband on the golf course, where she tends to feel far more competitive than her actual skill level would suggest.

You can follow Jo pretty much anywhere on social media (and she'd love it if you did!), but you can start at her website, jomcnallyromance.com.

Books by Jo McNally

Harlequin Special Edition

Gallant Lake Stories

A Man You Can Trust
It Started at Christmas...
Her Homecoming Wish
Changing His Plans

HQN

Rendezvous Falls

Slow Dancing at Sunrise
Stealing Kisses in the Snow
Sweet Nothings by Moonlight
Barefoot on a Starlit Night

Visit the Author Profile page
at Harlequin.com for more titles.

This book is dedicated to my nieces.
I don't say it often enough,
but I'm proud of the strong women you've become.
To Amy and Trista.

Chapter One

Monica clutched her broken arm to her side.
The old barn was in splinters all around her.
She was alone. The Shadow was gone. But
she'd learned long ago that monsters lurked
everywhere. This wasn't the end...just a pause.

Jillie Coleman sat back in her office chair after typing the last line of her latest book. She let out a soft grunt of surprise when her dog plopped her heavy head on Jillie's now-available lap.

"I know, Sophie." She scratched behind the Rottweiler's ears. "I never thought I'd finish this one, either."

Her editor would probably be thrilled to see a book delivered within two weeks of its deadline. Two weeks *after* the deadline. Still…that was pretty good for Jillie. Her agent would be less impressed, but she imagined Lisa would be secretly relieved it wasn't worse. She suspected both her publisher *and* agent adjusted their due dates to accommodate Jillie's love of the last-minute adrenaline rush that had propelled her through the past month. When she was pushing up against a deadline, that do-or-die feeling shoved all other thoughts from her mind. She had to live inside her fictional world. There were monsters there, but *she* was always the one in control.

She stretched, and her body popped and groaned in protest. She checked her smart watch, wincing at the time. She'd pulled an all-nighter without even realizing it. No wonder Sophie was staring up at her with those round, dark eyes, tongue lolling out in a sloppy grin, her butt wiggling back and forth on the floor. Sophie wanted her morning walk. Jillie stood, arching her back in another creaking stretch.

"I hear you, girl. The backyard will have to do for now. I need to get this manuscript sent off. And I need coffee. Not necessarily in that order."

Her office was in the lower back corner of her A-frame mountain home. It had been built in the late 1960s to serve as an upscale "camp" by the original owners. The family came to Gallant Lake to ski back in the days when the Gallant Lake Ski Lodge was open and thriving. But the old ski complex had been boarded up for a decade now, leaving the next generation of owners with an A-frame too remote and inconvenient to use. When Jillie saw it listed for sale four years ago, she knew it would be perfect, since *isolated* and very private had been at the top of her wish list.

She opened the back door and sent Sophie out to romp in the large fenced-in yard behind the cabin. The black-and-tan dog stopped at the bottom of the steps and looked back at her in obvious disappointment.

"It's this or nothing, dog. Go do your business. We'll take a proper walk together in a few hours, I promise."

Jillie made a pot of coffee and checked to be sure the manuscript file was complete with her most recent edits. It was still a bit draft-y, but it was a solid start and would give her editor plenty to work with. She hit Send, copying her agent and her assistant, Nia. With any luck, this second book in the Monsters in Shadow series would be released sometime in the following year. The only thing that moved fast in the publishing world was an author on deadline.

Sophie came back inside, staying close at Jillie's heels as Jillie ate breakfast and took a shower to wake herself up. She'd grab a long nap this afternoon, but there'd be no rest until this dog burned off some energy. Jillie pulled on jeans and a heavy

sweater against the chilly October air, laced up her
well-worn hiking boots and grabbed a knit hat. By
the time she zipped her jacket, Sophie was leaping
around her legs, whining and crying to get going.

It was a near-perfect fall day in Gallant Lake.
The foliage was at peak, or perhaps just past it, in
a showy palette of bronze, gold and crimson across
New York's Catskill Mountains. From the house,
she had spectacular views of the lake—and Gallant Mountain beyond it—through the triangular
two-story wall of windows facing east. When she
got to the base of the wraparound deck and stepped
onto the walking trail, the lake was nearly hidden.
It managed to peek through the trees occasionally
in all its sapphire glory.

Jillie imagined the streets in the village of Gallant
Lake would be crowded with tourists on a brilliant
Friday like this, especially right before a long weekend. She did a quick mental inventory of her pantry,
thankful she had no need to go anywhere near the
stores until next week. The sleepy town she'd loved
when she'd moved here was growing into a boom-
ing resort town. It was good news for the residents.
They'd been struggling to survive before the Gallant
Lake Resort had been refurbished by her friends,
Blake and Amanda Randall. The Randalls turned
it into a five-star destination for weddings, events
and of course, autumn-leaf-peeping. Luckily, most
businesses had survived the downturn caused by

the recent pandemic. They were bouncing back this year busier than ever.

The extra people made Jillie even more of a recluse. As far as she knew, no one—not even the locals—had ever recognized her as bestselling horror author J.L. Cole. She'd told a trusted few… *very* few. She threw a stick for Sophie to chase. But that wasn't her biggest worry. It was the press of people…*strangers*…that made her chest feel like it was in a vise when she was in town. So far she'd managed to deal with all the new people in Gallant Lake by watching her timing and relying on her friends. Winter was coming, which was always a quieter season.

Sophie barked at something up ahead on the trail. Jillie whistled, knowing the dog would never leave her alone for long. They were a few hundred yards behind the cabin now, climbing Watcher Mountain. No worries about wandering off the property, since the A-frame came with forty acres of mostly wooded land. Her neighbor to the north and west was the State of New York, so no worries about people building houses in the state forest. To the south was the abandoned ski resort. She'd heard it had been foreclosed on, but everyone figured the bank was going to be stuck with that wreck for a long time. The slopes were overgrown, the equipment was rusted in place and the lodge itself was looking shabby. Jillie basically had the mountain to herself—just the way she liked it.

She whistled again for Sophie, frowning when she didn't hear the dog crashing through the woods toward her as usual. There was another bark, from farther away. Jillie rushed ahead. If Sophie decided to chase after a deer, she could end up chasing it right onto state land. Bowhunting season for deer had started, and some hunter might decide to stop Sophie cold.

Jillie broke into a run, thankful she'd been faithfully hitting the treadmill at home. She heard another bark. Good, it was off to the south, toward the old ski resort. Being private property, there'd be less of a chance of hunters being around. Sophie sounded closer. And more agitated.

Jillie reached into her jacket pocket, making sure she had her can of bear spray handy. There were a good number of black bears in the Catskills. They were usually more active in the springtime, but it wasn't unheard of for one to wander through her woods. Black bears were far less aggressive than their western cousins, and could usually be scared away with a bit of noise as long as there weren't any cubs around. The time of year made cubs unlikely. Jillie was ready to defend herself and her dog. Sophie's barks were high-pitched and angry now, as if she had an animal cornered. Jillie sprinted up the trail and around a bend in the woods, giving a war cry as she got closer, just as she'd been taught by the local park ranger, Holly Avery.

But it wasn't a bear that Sophie had treed. It was a man. A tall stranger in street clothes and an overcoat, with thick waves of blond hair. Jillie did *not* lower the can of bear spray.

It was bad enough Matt Danzer was halfway up a damn tree, trying to escape some probably rabid killer dog. Now his humiliating situation was being witnessed by a crazed woman who'd just come screaming—literally—out of the woods at him. She had a knit cap on, and dark hair fanned out behind her as she ran at him. In her hand was the biggest can of pepper spray he'd ever seen. *Oh, crap...*

"Wait!" He held up his hand, nearly sliding out of the tree and into the jaws of the dog who was still baying at him. "Don't!"

She slid to a stop twenty feet away, her eyes wide, scanning the area as if she expected to see more guys in camel coats and dress shoes in the trees.

"Sophie…come." Her voice was low, but firm. The dog immediately stopped barking and trotted to the woman's side, casting Matt a malevolent glare every few steps. Clearly, this woman was not here for *his* protection. She gave the beast a look and Sophie sat abruptly next to her. The woman's shoulders slowly rose and fell as if taking a deep breath before she looked up at him.

"Who are you?" Unlike when she spoke to the dog, her voice was more than just firm. It was hard. On guard. And her hand still held that big-ass can of spray. Was that thing even legal?

"My name's Matt Danzer. Can you—" he gestured toward the can "—put that away?"

She looked at the spray as if she'd forgotten she even had it, then lowered her hand.

"You're trespassing." She looked at his attire, and he was pretty sure he saw a smile tease the corner of her mouth. "And you look ridiculous."

Matt grimaced. It had been his idea to drive straight to the lodge to inspect the new purchase after dropping his brother at their tiny rental house in Gallant Lake. Only to discover that he'd been hoodwinked. The website for the foreclosure auction said the old ski lodge needed "updating." The place was an overgrown disaster. This whole day had been a disaster. And that was *before* a giant dog chased him up a tree.

"I didn't expect to be…up here…today." He nodded at the dog, whose eyes hadn't left Matt for a second. "Is it safe for me to come down?"

"Sure. As long as you leave once you do. This is private property."

Matt slid toward the spot where the trunk split, then jumped to the ground. She flinched when he did—his first clue that she might be as frightened as she was angry. He stayed close to the tree, avoiding making direct eye contact with the dog, who was giving out a continuous low growl. He worked at keeping his voice as calm as possible.

"I'm sorry I alarmed you, but I'm actually the new owner of this property."

She stepped back. "You are *not*. This is *my* land. And the only other private property near here is the ski lodge, and it's in foreclosure."

"I know. I just bought it."

Her mouth dropped open. "You…you *couldn't* have…"

"Let me correct you. I *shouldn't* have. But I did. The bank put it on an online foreclosure auction, and I had a moment of bad decision making."

Understatement of the century. But it still might serve its purpose for his brother.

The brunette's dark eyes narrowed on him.

"I'll look into that, but I can assure you that we are standing on *my* land right now. You need to go."

The red-eye flight, the long drive from LaGuardia, listening to Bryce whining the whole way, the discovery that he'd bought a lemon of a ski resort *and* being chased up a tree all caught up with Matt's temper. "I don't even know who you are, lady. Why should I believe you about property lines?"

Her whole body went still at his sharp tone, and the dog growled more loudly. Both woman and dog were on edge. She straightened her shoulders and stood with feet apart and head high. A definite power pose, but he had a feeling it was just for show. Her eyes were wary.

"Who I *am* is the lady with the bear spray and the big dog." Matt hadn't forgotten about either one of those things. She rested her hand on the dog's head. "My name is Jillie Coleman. And this *is* my land." She nodded toward the direction he'd come from. "The property line is about thirty yards that way."

He frowned at that news. The gravel access road ran up this side of the property, and he remembered that the property line sort of zigzagged. But did the road? Which he was pretty sure was *less* than thirty yards away. This day got better and better. He nodded.

"Okay. I'll take a look at the survey and make sure I…"

"You don't need to check your survey!" Her voice cracked like a whip. "I know every inch of my property and I'm telling you that you're trespassing."

He held both hands up, keeping an eye on the agitated dog who was giving him the stink eye right now. Sophie was still sitting but was visibly trembling with the clear desire to tear him limb from limb. He took a slow step toward his property.

"I'll just be going now…" He took a few sideways steps, then swallowed hard and turned away. Jillie didn't seem the type to sic her dog on a retreating stranger. He hadn't gone ten feet when she blurted out a question.

"What are you going to do with the land?"

He faced her again, noting she was pocketing the bear spray at last. He wondered how many bears there actually were around here. He had the sense Jillie was extremely nervous, if not downright frightened, even though, as she pointed out, *she* was the one with the damn bear spray and a dog. She didn't want him there, but she wasn't running away. And now she was demanding answers. He gave her a reassuring smile.

"We're reopening the ski resort." Unless the lodge fell down first. "Hopefully, we'll have people on the slopes this winter. Do you ski?"

Jillie's expression fell so quickly he thought for a moment she was going to burst into tears. "Open it? To the *public*?"

"That's the general idea, yeah. But there's a lot of work to be done first."

Her face had gone white. Her shoulders fell. The dog looked up in concern, letting out a soft whine. Matt didn't know what to say to make her feel better. For some reason he wanted to try.

"I can make sure you and your family get free passes for the first season."

She blinked a few times, then seemed to force her body to straighten again.

"That won't be necessary. Just make sure you educate everyone, including yourself, on where the property lines are."

Her expression made it clear that she expected him to get moving, so he gave her a nod and turned away. He'd managed to annoy a neighbor in less than an hour—that was a record. He needed to find Bryce and check out the so-called "holiday rental cottage" he'd found online. Hopefully, that was in better shape than the ski resort he'd found the same way. He resisted the urge to look back at Jillie Coleman as he walked.

Matt flipped properties for a living, and never cared much what the neighbors thought while he was working. When they saw the end result and the positive effect it had on their property values, they were usually happy enough. But he did care when they acted as if they were afraid around him. His new neighbor was definitely afraid. And that didn't sit well at all.

Chapter Two

Monica should have known her peaceful sanctuary wouldn't last long. The Shadows were gaining power from the earth again. She was going to need help to stop them.

She was going to need the people who claimed to be her friends.

Jillie scowled at Mackenzie Adams, who'd just delivered Jillie's groceries, as well as half a case of booze from Mack's liquor store. Even though it was only ten in the morning, Jillie was tempted to open a bottle of vodka. She wasn't mad at Mack, of course. But she *was* angry and frustrated over the news Mack had delivered.

"So you're telling me there's nothing I can do about this guy trying to reopen the ski lodge?"

Mack pulled her honey-blond hair back and held it for a moment before dropping it. Her hair was as bright and thick as Jillie's was dark and fine. "It looks like he bought the property fair and square in a foreclosure auction a couple months ago. Dan checked, and the guy worked with the county on getting all the right permits after that. So he's basically cleared for opening as soon as the place is ready. Electricians and plumbers have already been over there working."

Mack married Gallant Lake's beloved police chief, Dan Adams, a month ago. While Mack had only recently returned to town to take over her dad's business, Dan had been here his entire life. Jillie liked the chief's steady, totally unruffled approach to his job. She also liked his deep loyalty to friends and family, including Mack and his young daughter from a previous marriage, Chloe. Jillie called Dan right after that Matt Danzer person walked away from her on the mountain a few days ago. She'd hoped to find the guy had broken some law—*any* law—but no such luck.

It was a raw, rainy day, and Mack quickly accepted the mug of coffee Jillie handed her, cupping her hands around it. Jillie started putting the groceries away. As small as the grocery store was in Gallant Lake, it was still too much for Jillie. Usually she ordered online and picked up her purchases curbside—a service that became easier and more common after the pandemic shutdown—but she had a great crew of friends here who would often offer to pick things up for her if they were coming to her place.

"Did Dan look extra deep into this guy, though?" she asked as she put a carton of eggs in the refrigerator. "Even if the *deal* is legit, that doesn't mean *Danzer* is. I mean, he *was* trespassing on my property."

Mack arched one eyebrow at her.

"From what you said, he—" she raised her fingers to make air quotes "—*trespassed* by less than fifty feet, told you he was mistaken about the property line and left when you told him to. That may be trespassing by the letter of the law, but is charging the guy with a crime really how you want to start your relationship with a new neighbor?"

Jillie scowled again. "I'm not going to *have* a relationship with the new neighbor. I don't even *want* a new neighbor. He'd better stay on his side of the line, or I *will* be charging him." She was tossing boxes of pasta into the cupboard with unusual force. She had a strange feeling Matt Danzer was the kind of guy who liked to push his limits. Which meant she'd have to keep a close eye on him. Exactly what she didn't want to do. "Dan didn't find *anything* shady about him? What kind of man wears a suit and a camel coat to climb a mountainside? Maybe he's part of the Mafia or something..."

Mack laughed, sliding a case of sparkling water across the island to her. "The Mafia? I know you don't like strangers, Jillie, but it's pretty unlikely that the *mob* is expanding to Gallant Lake." She took another sip of her hot coffee, sighing as she did. "I'm sorry. Dan says the guy is, and I quote, *squeaky clean.* He also said to remind you he's not supposed to be checking up on law-abiding citizens, so this conversation never happened, okay?" She waited for Jillie's nod of agreement. "Danzer makes his living as a flipper, but with businesses more than houses. He buys properties, spends time rebuilding them and relaunching the business, then he sells and moves on. He started in Colorado, but he's lived all over, mostly in ski towns." She leaned forward and lowered her voice dramatically. "Turns out his brother is none other than Bryce Danzer, the world champion downhill skier. You know, the bad boy of skiing that got all the press a few years ago?"

Jillie frowned. "That kid who got drunk at some party and missed his time slot for his team qualifier? There was a big dustup when they gave him another slot. People said he didn't deserve the second chance." Great, she had some privileged party boy and his probably doting brother moving in.

"That's the guy." Mack nodded. "He went on

to win the freakin' gold medal that year and went straight into rehab the next day. He's been in and out of trouble ever since. His competition record has been a roller coaster. Then he broke his leg on a practice run last spring. Rumor was he'd been drinking." She waggled her eyebrows and Jillie started to laugh.

"This report is a little more tabloid-y than I was expecting from Dan."

"I told you Dan didn't want to do any reporting at all. He gave me just enough information to do a deep dive online myself," Mack explained. "And Bryce was far more interesting than his big brother. Matt's a bit of a bore, at least online. He's managed his brother's career, which probably keeps him busy. He's single, by the way."

"As if I care," Jillie scoffed.

"Well, if I didn't have the best husband in the world, *I'd* be caring. I only found a couple pictures of him, but the man looks like a golden sun god."

"He didn't look very godlike when Sophie chased him up that tree the other day."

Except he kinda did, dressed in that ridiculous business getup, standing in the split of an old apple tree, staring at her can of bear spray and arguing that he wasn't trespassing. That thick shock of blond hair that fell across his forehead made him look like a movie star. Mack was staring at her in amusement.

"What?" Jillie sighed. "Okay, fine. He's pretty.

But you know I don't care about that." She closed the pantry door. "This is a disaster, Mack. If he opens that resort, there'll be people all over the place. How am I going to write? It's my worst nightmare. I'll have to move…"

"Whoa, whoa—slow down, girl." Mack set her coffee mug down. "You can't even see the slopes or the lodge from here. That means they can't see you, either. And yeah, there might be more traffic, but your place is hidden from the road, too." She reached over and took Jillie's hand. "We take care of our own in this town, and no one wants you to leave. If either one of these Danzer guys does anything to bother you, they'll have all of Gallant Lake to deal with."

Jillie's eyes went moist. Mack was right about Gallant Lake. About people taking care of her. They protected her from all the things that made her feel threatened, which was a pretty long list. They shopped for her. They delivered things to her. They provided safe places to gather and always showed her where the back doors and hidden exits were if she panicked.

Once Philadelphia had become unbearable because of its size and the memories and the chance of seeing *him* again, This town provided the refuge she'd needed. Her Philly friends laughed at the idea of her going from her downtown condo to a mountainside A-frame. But from the moment she'd seen this place, tucked deep in the pines at the end of a long driveway off a private road, she'd known it was her home. Her current book series was about shadowy monsters who gained strength from mountain stone. *This* mountain gave *her* strength. Made her feel safe.

"Oh, I almost forgot," Mack said, pushing away from the kitchen island and standing. "Dan wanted me to tell you that he and Asher will come up here in the next few days and make sure your property line is clearly marked with no-trespassing signs all the way up the slope." She reached for her jacket. "He'll text you before they arrive."

Her friends accommodated her phobias without question. A few of them had their own past traumas to deal with, so they got it. Even if she knew they were coming, they would text or call from the base of the mountain to let her know they'd arrived. If they forgot, the security camera alongside the driveway would alert her. Having friends in her own home was nowhere near as fraught with the threat of a panic attack as leaving her property. No matter where she was, she didn't like surprises. As Matt Danzer had discovered the other day.

She waved from the deck as Mack drove away. Knowing that Dan and Asher Peyton, husband of her friend Nora, would be putting up more posted signs made her feel better. There'd be no excuse for any future misunderstandings from the Danzer brothers or anyone else. She headed to her office in the back of the house and got to work. First up was checking social media and posting something—this week's share was a photo of Sophie stretched out on the sofa, with the background details carefully blurred. Jillie's publicist made her reclusive lifestyle part of her so-called *brand*, without ever addressing why J.L. Cole lived such a solitary life. It had become part of the mystique—a bestselling horror author who rarely, if ever, appeared publicly. But fans these days expected *something*, so she did a minimal amount of social media to stay in touch.

Many fans had guessed she lived in New England, but they usually speculated she was in the wilds of Maine, or maybe Vermont. Once in a while someone guessed the Adirondacks, a few hours north of her actual home in the Catskills. She'd been lucky. No one had been all that desperate to find her. She wasn't a mega-celebrity. There was just an idle curiosity that popped up occasionally. Her agent had warned that could change once the pending movie deal became official. It seemed so incredible that her little books—stuff she dreamed up in her head and tapped onto a keyboard—could end up on the big screen starring actors known the world around.

She pulled up her publisher's author-only website and reviewed some potential cover ideas for the final book. Fame and fortune had never been her goal in life. She just wanted to write stories. The process was cathartic for her. Most writers wanted people to see their work, of course, and Jillie was no different. She may not be able to handle crowds of people in person, but she loved looking at sales stats and seeing that readers appreciated her art. Right or wrong, a large readership was a validation of sorts.

The money was nice. She glanced around her office with the wide windows facing the trees between her and the ski resort. She liked privacy, but she wasn't looking to live like some reality-show survivalist, existing in the wild on twigs and berries or making her own clothes out of birch bark. She liked nice things, like the second espresso maker sitting next to her desk, saving her a trip to the kitchen. The raw silk drapes framing the window. The expensive ergonomic chair she was sitting in. Yes, money had its perks.

But she considered herself more *comfortable* than wealthy. The kind of money being bandied about in reference to the movies made her anxious. Maybe the studio would buy the books and never produce anything. She'd heard of that happening. The thought was oddly reassuring, and she was finally able to stop fretting and start writing…after one more look out the window toward the Gallant Lake Ski Lodge. She'd be keeping a close eye on that property line. And on the new owner.

"You're telling me the only option is to drive the trucks right up the ski slope?" Matt rubbed his hand down his face and bit back a frustrated sigh, clutching his phone tightly. "Yeah, I *know* we'd have to build a road first. In the middle of the slope, which is not gonna happen." The snowmaking machine supplier reminded him that there used to be an access road. He knew that. And after looking at his property survey from every angle, he also knew that a big chunk of the old access road was now on Jillie Coleman's land. There'd been some sort of verbal agreement between prior owners of both properties, but his attorney told him it hadn't been used enough to assume automatic right-of-way. Which meant he was going to have to pay her a visit. She hadn't been thrilled with the idea of the ski resort *existing*, much less allowing him to use her property.

After the call ended, he went back to work removing the cheap paneling someone had hung inside the lodge in what was probably a low-budget 1980s remodel attempt. The faux paneling had to go. Once he and Bryce got the walls down to studs, Matt decided to remove a few non-load-bearing walls to open up the place. The long, shiny pine bar on the slope side of the lodge would now be open to the lounge area surrounding the distinctive fireplace. The vintage hearth had somehow survived all the remodels through the years. It was straight out of the 1960s with the circular red-metal chimney hanging down from the ceiling above the round hearth in the center of the lounge. It gave the room a funky, retro feel, so it was a definite keeper. The hearth was surrounded by a circle of flagstone flooring that was still in good shape. The worn plank floors had enough character to keep, too. They just needed some sanding and stain to freshen them up.

A small dining area was on the downslope side of the lodge, with nice views of Gallant Lake and the mountains beyond it. Huge picture windows lined three sides of the lodge, and Matt had already contracted a company to replace them all with triple-pane windows of the same size. They were scheduled to be installed the same week that the solar panels arrived for the roof. A retro *look* was fine, but this would very much be a state-of-the-art, energy-efficient building when he was done with it.

He grabbed a pile of the old paneling from the floor and dragged it to the open sliding glass doors. A wide flagstone veranda wrapped around three sides of the lodge. He groaned as he heaved the paneling over the timber railing and dropped them to the parking lot below. His brother's voice let out a string of curses.

"How about giving a heads-up before you try to bean me with scrap lumber?" Matt peered over the railing to where his younger brother stood. Bryce had his hands on his hips. "Aren't you supposed to be Mr. Safety about work sites? I coulda been killed." He was a good twenty feet from the scrap pile.

Matt shook his head. "Dude, if you can't see that pile of lumber or the ropes I put around it to keep people from walking into the danger zone, then you deserve a knock on the head." His eyes narrowed. "You were supposed to be here an hour ago to help with this. Where the hell have you been?"

The two of them had always been opposites. Their parents used to laugh that they each had a child of their own. Matt, although he shared his father's name, got his tall, blond, blue-eyed looks from his mother. And Bryce was Dad's spitting image, with his wiry build, thick brown hair and dark eyes. The differences didn't stop at looks. Matt had always had a practical, industrious approach to life, while Bryce was a freewheeling party boy. At least, he *had* been, until he nearly got himself booted from the US team permanently for getting in trouble one too many times.

His brother jogged up the wide stone stairway to the veranda. "Where I've been is exactly where you wanted me—discussing our little road dilemma with the forestry service. I happened to bump into the local ranger last night at the pizza place, the Chalet."

"You mean the little townie dive bar? *That* Chalet?"

Bryce put his hands to his chest in mock innocence. "Hey, they serve pizza there. That makes it a pizza place. Anyway, there was a group of ladies at a booth, and one of them recognized me…"

Matt groaned, still stuck on the idea of Bryce hanging out at a bar. "Wasn't the whole idea to lay low and *not* get recognized? We don't need Bryce Danzer groupies crawling around this place. We had a whole conversation about this."

Bryce shrugged. "Coming here wasn't my idea. I never agreed to lock myself in my room. Besides, in a town this small, I think we're safe. *Anyway*, you wanted to establish contact with the forest service, and our local forest ranger was one of the ladies I met."

They walked inside the lodge as Matt tried to count to ten in his head. "All it takes is one social media post by someone, and your whole fan base will be headed this way."

"First, my so-called fan base isn't interested in a guy who won't even be competing this year." A shadow crossed Bryce's face. "And all the ski bunnies are in Europe or up at Killington, where the snow is." He swung his arm around the inside of the lodge. "Even if an entourage showed up, they'd take one look at this rat hole and turn right back around. So give me a freakin' break about fans right now."

Matt grimaced. He'd promised Bryce he'd stop lecturing him. The kid—check that—the young *man* was twenty-four. He knew Bryce missed his buddies on the ski circuit. They'd both heard all the rumors suggesting he was finished. Or that the injury hadn't been that bad and he was actually in rehab again. It hadn't been an easy year.

"Okay," Matt said with a slow nod. "I deserve that. Sorry."

Bryce, like Dad, couldn't hold a grudge for long. He looked around the lodge with a one-shouldered shrug.

"S'okay. Didn't mean to insult your rat hole... I mean...ski lodge."

"So you met the ranger?" Who, of course, was a woman; Bryce was a perpetual woman magnet. It made sense a female forest ranger would fall into his orbit. Bryce nodded, reaching into the small refrigerator behind the bar for two bottles of water. He tossed one to Matt.

"Yup. She's a salty one, too. Curiously immune to my charms at the moment. I'll keep working on her, though." Bryce stared out the window. "She refused to talk business last night but agreed to meet me for coffee today. She said she'd follow up on our request for a temporary road on forestry land. She also said we shouldn't expect a yes."

Ski resorts rarely owned all of the hundreds of acres they occupied. Much of the land was leased from state or federal governments. Most of Watcher Mountain was New York State forest land. Using existing slopes on their land was one thing. Removing trees to lay a new road was a big ask. At the very least, it would take a pile of paperwork and months of meetings.

Matt cursed under his breath. "I can't catch a break with this place."

Bryce winked. "I told you this was a bad idea."

"You said you wanted your own private slope to rehab on, and here you are. The price was right and we *both* agreed we could use the slopes this winter and flip the place after that."

"Yeah, but..." Bryce gestured widely at the walls down to studs and the debris strewn around. "I didn't know we were buying *this* much of a fixer-upper."

"Neither did I, trust me. But the price was right, and the building is structurally sound beneath the mess. The roof is good. The slopes are in decent shape. The lift doesn't look like it will take too much work. The biggest tasks will be replacing the snow-making machines and getting this interior work done by Christmas break." No way they'd be ready for Thanksgiving. He drained his water and flipped the bottle into the recycling bin. "Even with a late start, we'll make a little money before we flip it next year."

"You sure you want to sell it that quick?"

Matt turned in surprise. "That's the plan, right? You'll be back on the circuit next winter, so..."

"*If* I get back out there, I don't need a chaperone anymore."

"I'm your manager, not your chaperone."

Bryce's mouth opened and closed a few times, his

forehead furrowing. He finally blew out a typically dramatic long breath. "Maybe it's time for you to… you know…live your own life. You don't have to be responsible for me forever."

Matt had been the only parent figure in Bryce's life for the past fourteen years, and he couldn't imagine that changing.

"It's a little early to put me out to pasture. I'm thirty-four, not sixty-two." Matt put his hand on Bryce's shoulder. "If this is about your leg, the doctors all say you're going to be fine. We'll be back on the circuit next season. And even if I don't go on the road with you next year, do you really think Gallant Lake is the kind of place I'm going to put down roots in? It's not exactly Vail."

The move from Boulder to Vail years ago had been Mom's idea. Bryce flew down the slopes as if he'd been born to live on skis, and she saw his bright future before anyone else did. She wanted him to have every opportunity, and his coach at the time was in Vail. Dad was a tech consultant, so he could do his job from anywhere. They bought a little house in an older neighborhood. Bryce started winning junior Alpine events and never looked back.

"Uh…" Bryce's eyebrow arched. "You *hated* Vail by the time we left. You called it a vast wasteland of the rich, with the working class folks getting priced out of housing and…"

"Thank you. I remember what I said."

"Which is why you need a new place to settle that's different. It would be on-brand for one of the Danzer brothers to own a ski resort, even if it *is* a baby one."

Matt shook his head, staring up the overgrown slopes outside the window. "It won't even be a baby one if we don't get the snowmaking system installed. And we can't do that without a road. And the only road is on our very unfriendly neighbor's land." He looked toward the woods where he'd met Jillie Coleman. Or more accurately, where he'd been chased up a tree by her dog.

"They'll probably be reasonable if you go talk to them."

Matt wasn't all that sure. Jillie had been pretty combative the first time they'd talked. She'd been clear about *not* wanting the resort to open. But they needed that road. He rubbed the back of his neck. It wouldn't be the first time he'd taken a project neighbor to court if it came to that, but it was always a last resort. The idea of reaching that point with Jillie set him on edge.

"One way or another, Coleman's gonna have to give us access, or things could get ugly. I don't *want* to start a turf war with a neighbor, but…"

Bryce followed his gaze to the woods. "Like Mom used to say, sometimes it's better to ask forgiveness than permission. What could they do to us if we told the contractors to use the damn road?"

"They could have your asses tossed in jail."

The male voice had both brothers spinning on their heels. A uniformed police officer stood in the open doorway. His straight-brimmed gray hat sat squarely on his head, casting his eyes in shadow, but not disguising their chill. His arms were folded stiffly across his chest. This was one unhappy cop. Not exactly the way Matt wanted to start relations with local law enforcement.

Matt forced his mouth into a cheerful smile, trying to give a light laugh. It sounded as forced as it was. "Don't mind us—that was just wishful thinking…" No, that didn't sound good. "I mean, we weren't seriously planning anything…" Except it sure must have sounded that way. He stopped digging himself deeper and stepped forward, hand extended. "I'm Matt Danzer, and this is my brother, Bryce. We're the new owners of—"

"I know who you are." The officer hesitated, then took Matt's hand and shook it. He did the same with Bryce. "I'm Police Chief Dan Adams." He fixed Matt with a hard stare. "I helped nail up those no-trespassing signs on Jillie's property line yesterday. If you think you can just traipse over there again without permission, then you and I will be having a long chat. At the police station."

There was a heavy moment of silence. Matt looked up at the ceiling with a long sigh, his shoulders sagging. It was barely noon and this day was already off to a banner start.

"Chief Adams, I'm sorry. We were blowing off some of our frustration over the situation with our neighbor, and I know what you overheard must have sounded bad." From the way he said *Jillie's property*, it was clear the man knew her well, and liked her. Which meant Matt had to tread carefully. "I've only met Miss Coleman once, and I was on her property completely by accident…"

Bryce barked out a laugh. "Wait, I'm just now putting this together. Is *Miss Coleman* the lady who chased you up a tree?"

Something cracked in the police chief's stern expression. His eyebrow vibrated just a bit, as if it wanted to rise, but had been wrestled still. His mouth had the same struggle, but ultimately stayed straight after a little twitch.

"Jillie Coleman chased you up a *tree*?"

Matt flashed a dark look at his brother before answering. "It was actually that hellhound of hers that did it. Black beast was loose and treed me like I was a bear. Then Jillie showed up right with an actual canister of bear spray. I thought my first day on Watcher Mountain was going to be my last."

Bryce nudged the chief's shoulder. "Has he mentioned yet that we'd just arrived after flying into New York? That he was wearing a suit and an overcoat?"

Chief Dan Adams gave up any illusion of sternness and doubled over in laughter. "Jillie and Sophie chased you up a tree? While you were wearing a trench coat? Where the hell was *I* when this happened? Are there photos?" He was still laughing. *Great.* "No wonder she's not intimidated by you..." The chief's eyes closed, his laughter gone in an instant as he straightened. "Forget I said that, okay?"

"I wasn't trying to intimidate anyone." Matt frowned. What an odd thing to say.

"I'm sure you weren't. It's just that Jillie doesn't talk to strangers." His eyes were no longer chilly, and he looked around the lodge with genuine interest. "Everyone was surprised when we heard the old ski resort had sold. A lot of us natives remember coming here in our younger days. You're really gonna reopen it for skiing?"

This was more than casual conversation. Matt was being gently yet firmly interrogated.

"Skiing and snowboarding in the winter. I'm hoping to be able to repair that old alpine slide in time for summer, and add a couple of zip lines, too." The cement slide ran from almost the very top of the mountain down past the lodge. People rode on it by sitting on plastic seats with a braking bar to control their speed as they whizzed through the trees on the far side of the property. Some of the iron supports needed work, but that was a job for spring.

The chief's smile warmed. "Yeah, I've had some

wild rides on that alpine slide—you could really get flying. And zip lines up here should be a good draw with the views." He shifted his weight, taking off his hat and running his hand through his sandy hair with a sigh. "Are you and Jillie Coleman going to be a problem for me?"

And there it was. The thing the police chief most wanted to know.

"I honestly hope not, Chief. She didn't send you over here, did she?"

"Call me Dan. And no, not exactly. But she's anxious about the resort being sold. She wasn't expecting to have neighbors."

"Well, no offense, but that was an unrealistic expectation on her part. There were big plywood forsale signs at the bottom of the road. It's not like I did anything wrong."

Dan pursed his lips, staring at the floor for a moment. Whatever he was battling with internally, he seemed to resolve it with a nod to himself. He looked up. "No, you didn't do anything wrong. Why don't you show me around? I drank my share of beer up here in my young-and-crazy days. The last owners basically turned it into a year-round party house. Lots of booze and very little investment in the place."

Matt started a quick tour after motioning to Bryce to get to work hauling more paneling outside. They were on a tight schedule if they wanted to open for the holidays. He walked Dan over to the wall facing the woods toward Jillie's land. "I'm going to add more windows on this wall, so they wrap all the way around. This will be a tech center with a coffee bar. We'll have high-speed charging stations and lockers to stow customers' tablets and laptops. That way they can work or do their social media stuff in between ski runs."

Dan looked at the few narrow windows now on that side. "So you're opening up the wall that faces Jillie's place?"

"Well, I didn't know that when we drew up the plans, but yes. It's not like anyone can see her..." Matt paused, noticing a tall, sharply pitched green-metal roof barely visible in the trees. "Is that her place over there? What is it, an A-frame?"

Dan nodded. "Probably built by the same guy who built the lodge." He glanced Matt's way. "It *used* to be secluded."

"Oh, come on," he protested. "No one's going to notice that. *I* never even noticed it before now. I think her privacy is safe."

"What are you guys looking at?" Bryce joined them again, with three bottles of cold beer dangling from his hand. "Oh, that A-frame over there? It's pretty sweet. If you look from the roof deck upstairs, you can see it real clear."

Dan's right brow arched at Matt, who immediately protested. "I'm *not* the bad guy here." He took one of the beers Bryce offered. "At least I'm not building some housing development next door to her."

"I get that," Dan said, shaking his head when Bryce tried to hand him a beer. "I'm on duty. But it may take a while for Jillie to wrap her head around it."

Matt scrubbed his face with his hand. "I don't want a battle with the woman. I didn't intentionally walk onto her property." He took a long swig of beer. "What's her deal, anyway? Are you and her…?"

Dan grinned and shook his head. "I'm a happily married man as of thirty-five days ago. Jillie's a good family friend." Bryce had returned again, this time with a can of soda for Dan, which he accepted with a nod of thanks. "To be honest, you're lucky Jillie talked to you at all."

Matt coughed. "Are you saying that was her *nice* side? She must be a real…"

Dan brought him up short with a raised hand and firm look. "Jillie Coleman's one of the nicest people in Gallant Lake. *And* one of the most well liked. I don't advise bad-mouthing her to anyone around here."

Bryce chuckled. "It's kinda fun seeing my perfect brother chastised by the law for a change."

Matt stared hard out the window at the steep roof in the distance. He was a businessman. He was used to having problems to solve. This felt…different.

Jillie was a mystery shrouded in smoke. Not that they'd had a chance to really have a conversation, other than her yelling at him to *get off my lawn*, but he was usually good at pegging people fast. Putting them in the right category. Enemy. Friend. Bystander. There was something about her. She was quick to bristle, but that thread of fear and jumpiness she had said there was more to her than just being a cranky neighbor.

"I don't know her, so I shouldn't say anything," Matt said. "She wasn't exactly neighborly when we met, though."

Dan's head tipped slightly. "You mean when she found you on her property."

"Well…yeah. But I wasn't there on purpose."

"You know that's not a legal defense, right?"

Bryce laughed, but Matt kept circling back to something Dan had said earlier.

"Why are you so surprised she talked to me?"

Dan shifted, suddenly uncomfortable. "Jillie just…really values her privacy."

"Yeah, I get that, but why?"

Dan's eyes narrowed. "That's none of your business."

Matt held up his hand. "I'm only trying to figure out how to negotiate with her about using that access road. It's my only feasible option to get the slope work done. Any tips on what might work with her?"

Dan stared out the window. Matt wondered if he'd

get an answer at all. The police chief's shoulders slowly rose and fell. "Like I said, Jillie values her privacy, and she doesn't like surprises. Don't show up unannounced. I'll be honest—I don't think she'll ever approve having strangers on her property. Too much risk of unexpected encounters."

Matt thought again about how jumpy Jillie had been. "Why is she so paranoid?"

Dan grunted. "You know I'm not answering that, right?"

A mystery shrouded in smoke…

"How am I supposed to *not* show up unannounced when I don't know how to contact her? Do you have her phone number?"

Dan chuckled and set his hat back on his head. "I'm the police chief, not a social secretary. I'm not giving you her phone number. You know her address. Send her a note."

"A *note*?" Matt laughed. "You mean, like a hand-written letter? You're kidding, right?"

"Look, you asked for advice. You didn't specify you only wanted advice you wanted to hear." Dan held out his hand. "It was good meeting you two. I'll give you another piece of advice—get into town and meet some of the other business owners." He shook hands with Matt and Bryce. "The commerce club is pretty active in Gallant Lake. My wife, Mack, is on the board—she owns the liquor store here. And talk to Nora at the coffee shop. She's plugged into everything going on in town."

Bryce nodded. "I had coffee with Holly at the coffee shop this morning. I was *not* expecting a café Americano that good in this little town. No offense…" He cringed when he caught Matt's glower. "What? Oh…sorry. I didn't mean…"

Dan waved him off. "Gallant Lake looks sleepy at first glance. We're sort of in a rebirth phase, since the big resort remodeled and started drawing a more upscale crowd a few years back. That's someone else you should meet—Blake Randall. You know what? I'll talk to Blake and see if we can set up a get-to-know-each-other meeting over drinks some night." He turned to Bryce, amused. "You met Holly, huh? How'd that go?"

Bryce grinned. "Probably as well as you seem to think. She's as prickly as the plant she's named after."

Dan patted Bryce's shoulder. "Gallant Lake tends to attract strong-willed women. Holly takes her job as forest ranger pretty seriously. She knows almost every inch of these mountains. You weren't thinking she'd let you build a new road on forest land, were you?" He started to laugh. "Good luck with that, kid. She's even more stubborn than Jillie." He turned to go, then glanced back, his eyes bright with humor. "And the two of them are friends, so don't even think about playing one against the other. They've probably already compared notes."

Matt gave a loud groan. "In other words, we're screwed."

The police chief's shoulders were shaking as he walked away.

"Pretty much."

Chapter Three

It was ridiculously dangerous for Monica to be so close to the Shadows. But she needed to know their patterns of behavior. So she crept to her hiding spot and prayed they never discovered her alone in their territory.

It had been a couple of weeks since Jillie chased Matt Danzer off her property. It was wishful thinking to imagine he'd just pack up and leave Watcher Mountain, but hey—a girl could dream, right? She stared at the masculine handwriting on the card she held. He clearly hadn't left. And he wanted to talk.

The front of the card was a watercolor image of

Main Street in Gallant Lake, American flags snap-
ping in the breeze coming off the water. Colorful
clapboard businesses lined the street, with a few
brick structures in the mix. The little gazebo on
the waterfront was hung with bunting, and families
strolled the sidewalks. Jillie recognized her friend
Amanda Randall's artwork right away. Amanda had
donated the image to the commerce club to raise
funds to continue the beautification of downtown.
It was being sold on notecards and T-shirts all over
town.

Jillie received it three days ago. She could see the
indentation the pen made on the cardstock. It must
have pained Danzer to write this.

> *Dear Miss Coleman,*
> *I'm sorry our initial meeting wasn't under bet-*
> *ter circumstances. I want to be a good neigh-*
> *bor. Would it be possible to meet somewhere*
> *to try again? I'd very much like to discuss the*
> *old access road, which is partially on your*
> *property. I'm willing to pay any reasonable*
> *lease amount to use it this fall. My number is*
> *below if you'd like to call or text. Thanks in*
> *advance—Matt Danzer*

Her suspicions were right. He wanted to use that
old access road. Which was *not* going to happen.
She stared at the card a moment longer, blinking

away an image of intense blue eyes hidden behind a shock of golden hair. Why was she keeping this note? *Not gonna happen.* She tossed it back onto her desk. Not in the trash can. Not yet.

She got back to work with the outline for the final *Monsters in Shadow* book. There were sticky notes of different colors scattered across the large whiteboard on her office wall. Each color represented characters, both monster and human, in her series. The colors allowed her to visualize whether the book was balanced. She scowled at the blue notes. This Robbie character was being very pushy, showing up in scenes never meant for him. Monica wasn't written to need the help of Robbie or anyone else. Heroines didn't need some man swooping in to save them. Not in *Jillie's* books, anyway.

She'd been rearranging scenes for an hour when she was disrupted by what sounded like a dump truck depositing a noisy load of…something. Rocks, maybe? She'd heard it yesterday, too. Her curiosity propelled her out of her office. She needed to clear her head, anyway. She grabbed her phone and her jacket,snapping the leash on Sophie. There was no harm in seeing what they were doing over there at the ski lodge. Just to be sure they weren't anywhere near her property line *or* her access road. She led Sophie straight through the woods toward the sound. The wet leaves were slippery under her feet, but she wanted to get close enough to see what was happening.

No one was likely to describe her as confrontational, but this *was* her home. Besides, that's what the phone was for. If there was a problem, she'd call Dan Adams.

She got her first glimpse of the bulldozer while she was still hidden in the trees. Hard to miss the large yellow piece of construction equipment chugging its way up *her* access road. Well, it *would* be hers after it traveled another fifty feet or so. At the helm was none other than her supposedly *harmless* new neighbor, Matt Danzer. He was dressed more appropriately than their first meeting, wearing jeans, work boots and a faded Carhartt jacket over a dark Henley. His hair was the same—long and wavy on top, and looking as if he'd just raked his fingers through it. His head kept swiveling from watching where he was going to looking behind him. The blade of the bulldozer was pushing a pile of small gray stones up the long-unused roadway. She watched from behind a towering pine tree, knowing exactly where the road crossed onto her land.

It would happen just beyond the tall, dead remains of what had once been a massive tree—one of her favorites on the mountain. Now it was just a blackened trunk, about fifteen feet high. The leafless remains of the treetop were already beginning to decay at the base of the trunk. The oak had snapped after a lightning strike during a spectacular storm the previous summer. Jillie had been watching out the window and saw the fireball erupt. The roar of thunder had made the A-frame rattle.

The dozer slowed. Matt looked at the burned-out tree trunk and the bright orange no-trespassing sign Dan and Asher nailed to it last week. His shoulders fell. His gaze went from the road ahead to the tree and back again. She could feel the temptation he had to keep moving forward. Onto her land. But in the end, he shook his head and shifted the large, noisy piece of machinery into Reverse. At the bottom of the hill, another dump truck was depositing more stone in the corner of the parking lot.

The lodge looked better than she'd remembered. The overgrown grass had been cut. Just that clearing of grass around the lodge and on the slopes was an improvement, even if it was turning brown like mown hay. The property looked…cared for. A crew of workers scrambled around the building. One group was using a small scissor lift to raise new windows in place. Another crew was on the roof, installing solar panels. Jillie couldn't help smiling in approval. She'd covered the south-facing side of her roof with solar panels.

Matt hopped off the bulldozer to talk to one of the men working at the lodge. He gestured up the mountain in her direction. Even though she and Sophie were hidden in the trees, she instinctively shrank back. But when he gestured to the piles of crushed stone and then back up the mountain, she realized he was looking at the road, not her.

She heard Sophie's low growl an instant before she heard a stranger's voice coming from farther up the slope.

"The best paparazzi shots are from up higher, but you'll be trespassing to get them. I'm pretty sure you are trespassing right now."

The man's voice sounded somewhere between annoyed and amused. Not threatening. She frantically searched the forest in that direction, but didn't see him until he stepped out into a small clearing. He was young, maybe midtwenties. He had dark hair and a slight but powerful build. He gave her a weary smile before he spoke again.

"I get that you people are only trying to make a living, but if my brother sees you, you're toast. There's no story here, just a raggedy old ski lodge. And I'm just a raggedy old skier trying to recuperate in peace. So beat it, okay?" He took a step closer, and Jillie stepped backward. At the same moment, Sophie surged forward, snarling at the man. Jillie was usually sure-footed in the woods, but the rain-slicked fall leaves were like walking on ice. She caught her heel on a tree root and had to clutch the tree trunk to stay standing.

"Oh, damn…" The young man took a few more

steps in her direction. "Are you okay? Never seen a paparazzo with a guard dog before…"

"Stay back!" She gasped out the words, and he froze in his tracks. Sophie's growls changed to high-pitched barking as she looked between Jillie and the man who was obviously Matt Danzer's younger brother. Jillie let go of the tree trunk and straightened. "Sophie, quiet."

The dog immediately stopped, sitting close and leaning against her leg to calm Jillie. Ready to protect her at a moment's notice if needed.

"Wait…you're not from the press, are you? You're our neighbor. The one with the barely contained werewolf as a pet?" He looked at Sophie and grinned, nowhere near as intimidated by the dog as his older brother had been. "You're a good girl, aren't you?"

Inexplicably, Sophie's butt wiggled in the undergrowth as she wagged her stub of a tail at him. *Some guard dog, Soph.* Also inexplicable was the fact that Jillie was still standing there and not running back to the house. Or having a panic attack. She'd been caught by surprise—her biggest trigger. But there was something about this man, his quick smile and his relaxed bearing, that put her at ease.

"You're Bryce Danzer, right?"

"Guilty as charged." He folded his arms across his chest, leaning against a tree as if he didn't have a care in the world. "I thought you were someone from the press snooping around, but you're Jillie Coleman. The one who chased my brother up a tree."

A startled laugh bubbled up, and she put her hand over her mouth to try holding it back. "That honor goes to my dog, I'm afraid."

"So he really was in a *tree*?" Bryce tipped his head back and laughed loudly. "Did you take a picture, by any chance?"

"Uh…no. Sorry."

"Damn, that would've been awesome. Finally, something to hold over *him* for a change!"

"Do you not get along?"

Bryce straightened. "I shouldn't make it sound like that. Sometimes he takes his manager role too seriously is all." He brushed his hair off his face, the move reminding her of his brother.

"His manager role?"

"Now I *know* you're not paparazzi, Jillie… Can I call you Jillie?" She nodded. "You don't know the story of the good boy/bad boy Danzer brothers?"

She remembered her conversation with Mack. "Oh, right. You're the skier. A gold medal winner? The bad-boy brother?" She had a hard time imagining this guy being all that bad, but there was a bit of devil in his eyes. He took a deep bow to acknowledge her guess and she continued. "And your brother is your manager?" The good guy.

"For now." His voice trailed off as if he was lost in thought for a moment. "He also basically raised me."

Mack hadn't mentioned that detail, and Jillie didn't remember hearing about it. She'd love to know more, but Bryce was already moving on. "Anyway, it's fun to be able to poke fun at *him* for doing something embarrassing." Bryce looked down at Sophie again. "And he painted your sweet dog as a fire-breathing Cerberus. You're just a sweet girl, aren't you?"

Sophie's mouth dropped open in a wide smile, her butt wiggling again.

"Your brother wasn't quite the dog charmer that you are." Jillie let herself smile back at him. He was carefully keeping his distance, respecting her space. And while he seemed like the type who was always casual, she had a feeling he was making a point of maintaining such a relaxed posture, to keep her at ease. A thought slid through her writer's mind that he could also be some psycho killer trying to lull her into feeling secure. But she'd learned a while ago that her writer's mind tended to go off the rails when it came to making reliable judgment calls. "To be fair, Sophie was running off-leash that day and came up on him unexpectedly. She tends to be calmer if she's on-leash with me." That wasn't always the case, but for some reason she was defending Matt's side of the story. "Did you know he sent me a letter?"

"Yeah. The police chief told us it would be a bad idea to just knock on your door, so Matt went the snail-mail route."

A chill went through her. "You talked to Dan Adams about me?"

"More like he talked to us. He paid us a visit and warned us off bothering you. Which is what makes it so interesting that I found *you* spying on the lodge."

She straightened. "I'm not spying. I'm just… walking my dog."

He raised an eyebrow. "You were literally hiding behind a tree."

"I saw your brother driving the bulldozer this way and wanted to be sure he didn't trespass again."

Bryce looked down the access road, then back to her. "Did Matt ask you about leasing your portion of the road in his letter?"

"Yes, I did." Matt Danzer was twenty feet below them, standing near one of the property markers. He looked down and gestured toward it, making sure she saw that he was on his side. "I have no intention of trespassing again."

Sophie stood, growling. They say to trust a dog's instincts about people, but Jillie knew her dog might be picking up on her own tension. Something about Matt unsettled her, which unsettled her dog. Jillie's eyes narrowed. "You still have a penchant for sneaking around."

"It was unintentional. Again. I saw Bryce talking to someone and thought it might be some nosy fans of his. They're bound to hunt him down here eventually." He nodded to her hands. "No pepper spray this time, Ms. Coleman?"

She pulled her shoulders back and raised her chin.

"It never occurred to me that I'd run into the same threat twice."

His hesitation was there and gone so fast she almost missed it. His smile deepened.

"I don't know, I've heard there really are bears around here."

A ripple of fear ran up her spine, then fizzled. That was odd. Then again, this was a guy who'd hidden in a tree, so he wasn't exactly intimidating. And he wasn't technically a stranger anymore. But he still made her feel…something. Not fear. She couldn't quite define it. As long as he stayed over there, she could put on a brave front. She looked toward his feet, feeling playful for some reason.

"At the moment I'm not as worried about bears as I am snakes."

She bit back laughter when his body recoiled at her words. His brows gathered tightly together as he started looking at the ground around him. A-*ha*. The man was afraid of snakes. His brother started to laugh.

"She got you with that one, Matt. Hit your biggest fear on the first try, too. I'm impressed."

Matt continued scanning the leaf-covered ground as if he expected a giant anaconda to spring at him on Watcher Mountain. His voice thinned. "There aren't poisonous snakes here…are there?"

There was something empowering in being the one *less* afraid for once. Even after Sophie had chased him up that tree, Matt had managed to act superior. But that act was fading fast today, along with the color in his face.

"Actually, we *do* have timber rattlesnakes around here." His eyes went wide, and even Bryce started checking the ground around his feet. Jillie knew what fear could do to a person and didn't have the heart to inflict it on someone else. "But it's too cold for them to be moving around. They're usually starting to hibernate by now, so you're safe for the next five or six months."

Both men visibly relaxed. And they both maintained their distance from her. She wasn't sure if Dan had told them to do that, or if they instinctively knew she was more comfortable with some space.

"About that road, Miss Coleman…um… Jillie…" Matt started. "I'm just looking for a way to move the contractor's equipment up the mountain over the next few weeks so they can get to the summit and work on the lift and install snow machines." She swallowed hard. She absolutely hated the thought of random strangers working around her place. He rushed on, probably noticing her hardening expression. "I *need* this road." He looked up the mountain again, heaving a large sigh. "I'll add a new road on the south side of the slopes, but I don't have time to do that before ski season starts. I've barely got time to do *anything* before then." He turned his intense blue eyes her way. "The old lift needs repair, and I'm putting in new snowmaking machines. The workers won't be able to get up there without using this road. I'll pay you…"

"It's not for sale."

"No, I mean I'll pay you to use it… I'll lease it from you until I can come up with another plan."

It wasn't an unreasonable offer. She glanced at her phone to check the time. She'd already lost too much writing time talking with the Danzer brothers. If there were trucks and tractors going up and down this path every day and disrupting her, she'd get *nothing* accomplished. Forget being a few weeks late—she'd *never* finish the book. She shook her head adamantly.

"No. It's not for lease. It's not for sale. It's not for public use. Period."

His mouth dropped open. "But…it's in the middle of the woods. The road's already sitting here." He brightened. "In fact, I can guarantee you we'll leave it in better shape than it is now. I'll fill the ruts and level it off. We can even add a layer of fresh gravel. This will be the prettiest private road you ever saw…"

"It's not up for negotiation. I said no, and I'm not changing my mind."

"Why the hell not?" His fingers curled, then straightened against his thighs.

"Matt…" Bryce warned. Jillie talked right over him.

"Because it's *my* property!" She gestured up the mountain. "And I can do what I want with it. And what I want is to *not* have noisy construction equipment disturbing my work."

He scrubbed his hands down his face in frustration, staring up at the bright blue sky dotted with cotton-ball clouds. She jumped when he clapped his hands together as if he'd just had a brilliant idea, flashing her a bright smile. "Okay, so you don't want to be disturbed. I take it you work from home. I know what it's like to work from home. We can solve this. What if…"

Jillie stiffened. "Any *solution* that involves your contractors coming on my land is a nonstarter."

His face fell, taking his smile with it. She almost felt sorry for him, as he'd clearly assumed she'd just accept whatever he was going to propose.

"Jillie, I…" He took a few steps toward her, but stopped when Sophie growled. "Don't you think you're being a little unreasonable here? I'm not asking to parade equipment up to your front door. I only need to use the road for a month or so." He leaned to the side and looked past her. "I can't even see your house from here, so how bad could it be…?"

"Look, *not* trespassing on my land may be inconvenient for you, but that's not my problem." She gestured to the lodge below them. "So you may as well get to work on a plan B."

He glared at the ground, and she could see a muscle ticking in his cheek. It was wildly uncharacteristic for her to put herself in a situation where she was facing down two strangers alone in the woods. Her grip on Sophie's leash tightened, and the dog responded by leaning tight against her leg, growling at Matt again.

Anger flared in his eyes. "What are you going to do, sic your dog on me?"

"Chill out, Matt." Bryce walked toward his brother. "This isn't the way to do it. We'll figure something out that works for everyone." He winked in Jillie's direction. Bryce's charm didn't send the same electrical energy across her skin as Matt's did. "And if not, we go to plan B, like Jillie said. In the meantime, pull in the Big Bad Wolf routine and walk away."

Matt threw his hands up. "We don't *have* a plan B! And the snowmaking machines arrive next week."

Bryce put his arm over his brother's shoulder and turned him away from Jillie.

"Then I guess we'd better come *up* with a plan B…after your temper cools, bro. I'm the hothead, remember?" Bryce called back to her as he walked away. "Nice to meet you, Jillie Coleman!"

Matt just grunted, glaring over his shoulder at her without saying a word.

That weird prickle of energy swept over her again. An angry man normally sent her running... or even collapsing. There was something about this particular angry man that didn't frighten her as much as...amuse her.

"Thanks, Bryce," she called out. "Oh, and good luck with that road problem, Matt!"

Matt opened his mouth, but Bryce gave his brother another firm tug downhill, still laughing loudly.

"You always told me to accept defeat with dignity, big brother, and walk away."

"Do you really think this will work?" Matt was pacing inside the Gallant Brew coffee shop on Main Street.

Nora Peyton, the owner of the shop, folded her arms and gave him a pointed stare.

"Not if you stalk around my place like an angry bear. Sit *down*, Matt."

"What if she doesn't show up?" He pulled out a chair in the empty café and threw himself into it.

Nora's husband, Asher, was leaning against the exposed-brick wall that ran the length of the place. He owned a furniture-making shop next door, but both businesses were closed right now. This top-secret meeting had been set up by the Peytons after

Matt had followed the police chief's advice and reached out to local business owners. After a few shared glasses of bourbon with Asher in his shop a few nights ago, Matt had agreed to meet Jillie Coleman in a so-called neutral setting. He knew the woman was nervous, but this amount of precaution seemed excessive.

Asher pushed off the wall, walking over to his petite wife and scooping her up for a quick but intense kiss before answering Matt.

"Relax, man. Try to remember you need *her*, not the other way around."

Matt nodded, pressing his lips into a tight line. "Trust me, I know how much I need her. I've pushed the work back as much as I can afford to. We've already had a couple snow flurries. If we get any real snow, I'll never be able to get the work done." He blew out a long breath and stretched, doing his best to get the tension out of his shoulders. "Ironic, right? I need snow, but not until we're ready for it. And Jillie Coleman is the key to everything." He gave Nora a reassuring smile. She'd been eyeing him with a healthy dose of suspicion all night. "I'm not an ax murderer. I'm not going to stalk the woman or…"

He sucked in a sharp breath, feeling a lightning bolt of clarity. Maybe it was all the worry about the lodge and his brother that made his brain so slow to catch on before now. Jillie's jumpiness. The shadow of caution that was always there in her eyes, even when she was joking with Bryce. Her refusal to meet with Matt at her home or at the lodge. She'd insisted on this happening somewhere familiar to her. Where her friends could be present for support. For protection. A chill wormed its way through his veins, and he turned to Asher.

"Something happened to her."

It wasn't a question. No wonder the police chief had been so proactive in warning him and his brother away from her. It wasn't because she was a prima donna. It was because she was a *victim*. The carefully blank looks Asher and Nora gave him confirmed it. "Someone hurt her. That's why she's so isolated. So careful. What happened?"

They shook their heads in unison, and Asher replied. "Not our story."

Nora added, "And not your business." She hesitated, and her voice softened. "Jillie is one of the smartest and strongest people I know."

Matt slumped against the back of the chair. He'd been looking at this all wrong. Jillie Coleman wasn't flighty and irresponsible. She was doing what she thought she had to. He looked up at Nora.

"But she needs to feel safe." Another hesitation, then she nodded. Her expression was less adversarial toward him. He turned the handle on his mug of coffee back and forth, watching the murky black liquid swirl inside. A lot like his feelings right now. Before he could ask any of the many questions he had, the back door opened. Mackenzie Adams from the liquor store came in, followed by Jillie.

The two women were quite a contrast. Mack was a tall, buxom blonde with a quick smile and, he'd learned, an equally quick wit. Jillie was petite, with softer curves and dark, straight hair. That hair was loose tonight, swept back off her shoulders to fall like satin down her back. Her eyes swept the interior of the café, and Matt realized why Nora sat him in the corner, against the wall. With Jillie coming in the back, it gave her plenty of space, and she had multiple escape routes. She could be out the front or back doors in a flash. The setup must have met with her approval, and she walked over after nodding at Nora's offer of a cup of tea.

She pulled out a chair and sat. Everything in her body language screamed she didn't want to be there. Her shoulders were high and tight. He could see the cords in her neck, tense and taut. Her jaw moved back and forth like a saw blade. His mind spun, trying to think of the best approach to put her at ease. Not to get what he wanted, but to make her feel safe. That was suddenly, and inexplicably, his top priority at the moment. In a normal business meeting, he'd be leaning forward and making firm eye contact, but that felt like a mistake. He could hear Bryce saying *this isn't the way.* So he made himself stay slumped back against his chair. Made sure his shoulders stayed relaxed. Kept turning his coffee mug. He gave her a quick glance of acknowledgment, then spoke to the mug.

"I've gotten us off to a really bad start, Jillie, and I'm sorry. I want you to know that I'm not here to try to talk you into anything." He looked over her shoulder to Asher, Nora and Mack. Jillie's guardians. He gave them a smile. "I appreciate your friends coming up with this idea to meet in neutral territory, but I want you to understand that *all* territory is neutral for us. This isn't a battle. We're not enemies. And I'll abide by any decision you make."

Sure, it would cost extra to get equipment up the mountain without the road, but it wasn't the budget breaker he'd been making it out to be. It would eat into his "unexpected expenses" fund, but that was what the fund was there for. After all these years of flipping properties, he'd learned there was always something. And the ski resort's *something* was the quiet brunette sitting in front of him. Her friend squad glanced at each other in surprise. Nora beamed at him like a proud mama hen.

Jillie considered his words, then gave him a level look. "I appreciate you saying that, but…I don't think you're going to change my mind." She gave Nora a quick smile of thanks when she delivered her cup of tea. "I value my peace and quiet."

Matt's hand curled into a fist against his thigh. He hated the thought that someone had hurt her enough to send her into seclusion. But he had to at least make his proposal, since that was the whole reason behind the meeting. He had a feeling she wasn't a woman who wanted pity. He cleared his throat gently.

"I understand you work from home and don't want to be disrupted." He wondered what kind of work she did. "What if I limit the hours the contractors use the road? I promise you they will not set foot off the road. They'll head right to the mountaintop without stopping on your property." He could see the slightest softening in her posture. She was considering it. He pressed on, careful not to sound too confident. "Is there a time of day that would be easier for you to have the trucks there? What if I had them go up between nine and ten, and then come back down between three and four? I could ask them to take everything they need in one trip up…but it might be multiple vehicles at once. Then just one trip down. Would that work? I'd pay you a lease, of course."

He threw that in, but Matt had a feeling money wasn't the issue. Not only because she hadn't responded before to his offers to pay her. He'd seen enough of the après-ski crowd to know expensive clothing and jewelry when he saw it. Her sweater and slacks were casual, but they looked like… money. She wasn't wearing much jewelry, just a simple necklace and earrings. A chunky ring with a dark red unpolished stone. None of it was costume jewelry.

"I can't believe I'm saying this," she started, glancing over at her friends, "but…how long a time are we talking? Days? Weeks?"

Matt kept his voice steady, trying not to sound eager or pushy. "Weeks. Three or four at most. I'll make the crews work around you." He thought about Dan warning him not to show up uninvited. She didn't like surprises. "I can text you every day when they're headed up, and again when they're coming back down. No surprises."

Silence hung in the room like fog. He couldn't see through it. Couldn't determine if it was in his favor or not. Jillie sipped her tea before nodding.

"I suppose that could work." She paused. "I know the ski lodge could help local businesses this winter if it's successful, and I don't want to stand in the way of that." She looked up at him through long, curved lashes. "I want you to donate any lease money you would have paid me to the commerce committee in Gallant Lake. They're helping businesses that were hit hardest by the pandemic."

"I'd be glad to." His words raced. "And this is only temporary, Jillie. Just until we can get another road built on the other side of the main slope next spring. I won't lie—it'll be busy for a month or so. We have to install new snowmakers and fix the old lift…"

Her eyebrows lifted and she smiled.

"Are you trying to talk me out of this?"

He huffed out a laugh. "God, no. But I want to be up front with you."

She looked into his eyes, then pulled up the small purse she'd hung on the back of the chair. She removed a thick ivory business card with embossed black lettering, sliding it across the table. "Here's my contact information. I'm trusting you to keep this confidential."

"Keep the agreement confidential?" He frowned in confusion.

"My personal information. Our mutual friends seem to think you're reliable, even though they just met you."

Their *mutual friends* seemed stunned at what had happened. They looked at each other, then back to Matt and Jillie. Mack was the first to speak up. "Just so you know, my husband is the one who trusted you first, and it would be a really bad idea to disappoint the police chief."

"I would *never*," he assured them before turning back to Jillie. "You can *all* trust me."

He put his fingers on the card but could see she was still tense. He waited until she nodded her head in approval before picking up the card. It was rich-looking, but simple. Her name. Her address. A phone number. An email address that was clearly a shadow account—WatcherMtWatcher at Inmail.

He handed her one of his own thin and slightly smudged business cards. "Sorry, I'm using ones I printed at home for now. I ordered some real cards for the ski lodge the other day."

Her lips went thin and tight as she looked at it. Her voice dropped so low she was almost talking to herself. "The ski lodge next door."

"Neighbors, Jillie." He extended his hand across the table. "Maybe friends?"

She stared, then accepted his hand and shook it before quickly releasing it. Behind her, Mack and Nora were both wide-eyed. Her hand was small in his. Warm. Trembling. He missed it as soon as she pulled away. She lifted her chin.

"Let's leave it at *neighbors*." She stood. "But there is no need for us to be uncivil."

He rose with her but stayed on his side of the table. "Do you want me to call or text when the workers are headed up the mountain?"

"A text will be fine. If I'm writing, I may not answer, but I'll hear it come in. No need to text twice." She paused, and he realized that was probably the most sentences she'd strung together at once while talking to him. And she'd revealed something of herself.

"You're a writer?" That fit with her working at home.

She paled. "Yes." She opened her mouth as if to

say more, then closed it again, turning to Mack. "Are you ready? I need to get back."

And just like that, she was gone down the back hall without a backward glance. Mack gave him an amused wave and followed. Matt thanked Nora and Asher for keeping the coffee shop open for the detente.

Nora smiled as she locked the front door and started turning out lights. "It went surprisingly well, I thought."

Asher agreed. "It felt like a declaration of peace. And you got what you wanted."

As Matt drove back to the rental house he and Bryce shared near the lake, he thought about that. He got what he wanted for the lodge.

But he found himself wanting more. Wanting to *know* more. About Jillie Coleman.

Chapter Four

The sun rose, looking very much like the literal ball of flame that it was. Sure, it brought warmth and light. But too much of anything was dangerous. Monica rubbed her eyes and sighed. Maybe that Robbie guy in the resistance was right. Maybe she was too skeptical. Look at her—she was suspicious of the sun.

Jillie leaned back in her chair with a satisfied sigh. Even after writing ten books, having a good writing day still felt like a precious gift. She'd stalled out for a while after discovering Matt Danzer in a tree a few weeks ago, but she was beginning to find her writing mojo again. As unhappy as she was at the thought of her mountainside haven being disturbed by a commercial property right next door, the truth was next door was far enough away where it didn't have to disrupt her routine.

Even with the leaves off the trees, she'd been barely able to see the trucks lumbering up the mountain every morning. Matt had held to his promise, texting her before they headed up and again when they were done for the day. That didn't mean it had gone smoothly. Whenever they veered off the routine, she'd text Matt to let him know. After all, a deal was a deal. And to be honest, it was kinda fun.

The first few days after they'd started last week were the bumpiest. The workers weren't on time. Matt forgot to tell her about changes to the schedule. The contractors didn't always notify Matt when they needed to go back down the mountain for tools or whatever. It led to some testy text conversations between Jillie and Matt.

They're early...

Okay, I didn't know...

You'd better know the next time...

Yes, ma'am.

Don't call me ma'am.

What then? Hey, lady?

Ha ha. Jillie is fine.

Yes, ma'am.

She'd groaned at that. He thought he was some kind of comedian now. The weekend had been quiet, but on Monday someone had driven a pickup truck down the mountain without warning around noontime. She'd texted Matt, and he'd responded tersely that the contractor forgot some tools and would be heading back up again shortly. Jillie had replied that wasn't part of the agreement, and he'd apologized. Just one word—*sorry*. She was going to reply with something snarky, then deleted it. It was hard to tell from a text, but she had the feeling he wasn't in a joking mood.

On Tuesday there was a horrendous screeching sound on the mountain that had jolted her out of her chair and startled Sophie. The sound happened again, and she promptly texted Matt. They hadn't discussed noise at their little detente summit at Nora's, but the whole point of the agreement was that she wouldn't be disturbed. It had taken a while, but Matt had texted back about the noise.

Working on the damn lift. The thing is rusted all to hell.

She'd stared at the words in consternation. He hadn't addressed the problem.

You said I wouldn't be interrupted during the day.

His response had been swift.

Our agreement was about using the road. This isn't about the road. It'll get quieter.

She'd narrowed her eyes at the screen.

If it doesn't, I may rethink our agreement.

By the time she'd hit Send, she regretted the tone. She was coming across as a crank.

I'm on it. Ma'am.

She grinned. Playful Matt had returned.

The high-pitched squeal of metal on metal *did* disappear by the end of the day.

On Wednesday, the issue was more manageable, but Matt's playfulness had vanished again. The workers forgot to let Matt know they were coming down early, so he wasn't able to warn her about the vehicles rumbling down the mountain. She'd answered his explanation with a reminder that he'd promised no surprises. His response told her Matt might be regretting their agreement at this point.

Srsly?

There was no doubt he was getting annoyed when she texted on Thursday and asked why only one truck had gone up the mountain that morning. There were usually anywhere from two to four vehicles. Matt's text had oozed with irritation.

Is that a question? A complaint? Is there some specific number you were expecting?

He was definitely annoyed. And it seemed he was having a bad week. Jillie was really out of practice with this whole negotiate-with-strangers thing. She was bad at it, and had a feeling she was getting on Matt's last nerve.

It's a fair question. Just wondering if there will be stragglers going up later.

It took a moment for Matt to respond. That made her smile for some reason. This was becoming a game. She didn't play games. At least, not until now. She finally saw bubbles wavering on the phone screen.

The work on the lift is done, so that crew is gone. The electricians are the only ones working today and tomorrow.

She could see he was typing something else.

Would you like me to give you a vehicle count daily?

She didn't need that, of course, but she couldn't resist.

Yes, please. Thanks for offering.

He didn't respond, but she could picture him muttering a few curse words as he read her reply. Friday—so far—had been uneventful. His morning text had been strictly factual. Just a quick message that a one-vehicle crew was heading up. Oddly enough, the back and forth all week with Matt had energized Jillie. She'd started timing her days around them, using the morning text as her signal to stop writing—which she usually started early—and grab another cup of coffee. Then she'd write until around one, eat a light lunch, take a walk with Sophie and do business tasks if she had any—emails, social media, phone calls. She tried not to spend more than an hour on that stuff before she got back to her writing for a few more hours. Once she got Matt's daily afternoon text letting her know the crew was on their way down, she'd break for dinner and relax for the evening with a good book or movie.

But today she'd already stopped writing when Matt's text came through that the workers were finished for the afternoon and were leaving. He'd followed it up with a sarcastic still just one vehicle. *It made her laugh.* She'd just completed a pivotal scene in the book and liked the result, so she was in a good mood. She wasn't going to push her luck by picking a fight.

She'd done some cleaning and organizing in the kitchen. She called out to Sophie after hearing the truck go down the access road. The big dog was stretched out on the floor by the ceiling-high windows in the great room, soaking up a bit of early November sunshine. Sophie scrambled to her feet, going from sound asleep to *let's go!* as soon as Jillie picked up her leash.

Sophie was an emotional therapy dog dropout. She'd been trained to detect and alleviate anxiety attacks, which she was good at. She could sense Jillie's moods, and would notice nervous reactions like Jillie rubbing her legs over and over or rocking back and forth. Sophie would get right in Jillie's face to distract her, making eye contact. The closeness would slow her breathing to match Sophie's.

But a certified therapy dog needed to accompany their human in public places, and Sophie had proved to be too…enthusiastic…for that. She was easily distracted in crowds or shops, especially as a young dog in training. She'd wanted to play. Instead of fetching a cell phone and delivering it to her human to call for help, she was more likely to run away and chew on it for a while.

Sophie's inability to behave in public spaces was no problem for Jillie, since she avoided public spaces, anyway. When her assistant, Nia, saw the school's ad online three years ago, offering "semi-therapy" dogs that hadn't quite made the grade, she'd sent the information to Jillie. And Sophie had arrived a month later, a headstrong adolescent pup who'd taken one look at Jillie and bonded immediately. The feeling was mutual. Sophie gave her a reason to get up and move, and she felt safe with the dog at her side. It was good to have someone to be responsible for. Someone to keep her company. Someone to bark at her, like Sophie was doing right now, to get her out of her head and out the door.

They headed up Watcher Mountain, sticking to familiar paths. The sun was setting, reminding her that days were rapidly getting shorter. There had already been a few light snow flurries, but nothing had accumulated. November was upon them, though, so it was only a matter of time. She pulled her jacket tight against the chilly wind. It was time to break out her real winter gear, like the down vests and heavier sweaters. Sophie was off-leash, running up ahead, when Jillie came to an abrupt stop. Were those voices she heard behind her?

There were definitely people talking, and it sounded like a *group* of people. On *her* mountain.

She called out to Sophie, who'd run on ahead, then pulled her phone out. It had to be more of Matt's workers. That was the only explanation. Except the sun was setting and it was getting late for any work to be accomplished. Maybe they forgot something again.

Did your workers come back up the mountain?

At first, she didn't think he was going to answer.

Relax, okay? They're done for the week.

She frowned. That didn't make sense.

Then who's on the mountain? I hear voices.

His answer was swift and annoyed.

Not my people. Not my problem.

She may have carried their little game too far, which is what happened when you didn't have much practice at playing. He thought she was being a pest. There was a burst of laughter from down the trail. Those people were on her land. Between her and the cabin. Had someone found out where she lived? Who she was? Her chest tightened, squeezing her lungs and quickly making breathing difficult. Sophie was at her side now, leaning into her leg with a soft whine. Jillie started dialing Dan's number when another text chimed in from Matt. And another.

You okay?

I'm at the house. Where are YOU?

He was at the house? *Whose* house? More laughter came from down the trail—male and female. Young. They weren't workers. Maybe a group of trespassing hikers? High school kids goofing off? Or J.L. Cole fans looking for their idol. It didn't matter. She was trapped. She turned to go higher, Sophie at her heels. The trail was steep this high up, and climbing required breathing. Her lungs were *not* cooperating. Still she climbed, her eyes focused firmly on the summit. She'd be safe there. That was all she could think. *Get to the summit.* She couldn't hear the voices anymore, but that didn't matter. *Just get to the summit.* She was beginning to think like Monica in her books—the mountain meant danger. It had always been Jillie's strength.

She stumbled when her phone rang. She'd forgotten it was still clutched in her hand. That was right… she was going to call Dan. Too late now. Only the summit would help. But she swiped the screen, anyway, breathing out a quick "What?"

Matt's voice was almost as breathless as hers,

as if he'd been running, too. "They're gone. Just a bunch of damn kids hoping to see Bryce. Where are you, Jillie?"

"Up the mountain with Sophie." Her panic was pushing her forward, even after learning the danger was past. She never saw the tree root jutting across the trail. She went down with a thud and a curse. Sophie barked, then rushed over to lick Jillie's face and make soothing eye contact, just the way she'd been taught.

"Jillie? *Jillie!*" Matt's voice was yelling through the phone, which had landed a few feet ahead of her. But she could also hear him below her on the trail. He was close. Sophie pushed against her chest, remembering her training. Close contact. Heart to heart. Slowing Jillie's breathing enough that she was able to call out.

"I'm up here!"

Matt thought he was in pretty good shape, but running full-speed up Watcher Mountain had his lungs on fire. The adrenaline from his anger and panic hadn't helped. He'd *told* Bryce to lay low, but the damn kid never listened to him. He'd been hanging out at the Chalet at night, and word had gotten out to a few ski groupies in the area who'd recognized him. They'd been trying to sneak over to the lodge using the trees to hide their progress. He'd sent them hurrying back down the mountain to their cars after lying and telling them the cops were on the way. And convincing them that an Olympic gold medalist would never be hanging around a run-down ski slope like this one.

Then he'd dashed up the trail, looking for Jillie before darkness descended completely. Hearing her voice through the trees sent a wave of relief through him. He came around a curve in the trail and saw her sitting on the ground. That hellhound of hers was lying across her lap, as if trying to physically console her. Jillie's hand moved absently in the dog's fur. She flinched when she saw him. He slid to a stop, holding his hands up in innocence.

"Jillie, it's me. Are you hurt?"

The dog snarled and barked at him but didn't leave Jillie's lap.

"Shush, Sophie." Jillie's hand on the dog's head silenced her. "I'm okay. I just…need a minute…"

Her chest rose and fell unevenly. She was wide-eyed and pale, her body twitching slightly every few seconds. Her eyes glimmered with unshed tears. She was about two seconds away from a meltdown. Matt remembered something from his teen years and abruptly sat about fifteen feet away from her. Her head lifted. Even the dog stared at him in confusion.

"Wh-what are you doing?"

Matt shrugged. "When Bryce was small, he'd freak out if our parents left for a night out. He'd scream and sob and beat on the door after they left.

It was full-drama hysterics. The more I tried to settle him down, the worse he got. One night I sat down on the floor and started playing a board game by myself. Without a participating audience, he calmed down in no time at all, and eventually came to join me, sniffling away his tears." Matt gestured between them. "I figure I'm less threatening to you at this level, so I'll just wait until you're ready." He looked around the dark shadows under the pines. "It's gonna be dark soon, but I have a flashlight in my pack, so take your time."

He slid the small backpack around to his lap and patted it. It was basically an emergency kit—a habit he'd started when Bryce was even more of a loose cannon than he was now. It wasn't unusual a few years ago to get a late-night call that he'd been doing something stupid with his friends and got hurt or got caught or needed to escape from some girl's house before her parents—or husband—got home.

Jillie stared for a moment, then shook her head slowly. Some of the tension eased from her shoulders. "I'll ignore the suggestion that I'm acting like a toddler, and just say…thank you. For coming here. For getting rid of the people. For…" She gestured toward him, her voice still strained, but a smile playing at her lips. "For sitting down and telling me to take my time."

"Those kids…" They'd been older teens, maybe a few in their young twenties. They'd seemed sober and genuinely curious. Then again… "They didn't hassle you, did they?"

She shook her head, staring at the ground. "I don't think they had any idea I was here. Are you sure they were looking for Bryce? Not someone else?" She blew out a soft breath. "When I heard them I just… freaked out. As you can see." She gestured to herself.

"Totally understandable. You're not much for trespassers, as I well know." Her smile reached her eyes, and he felt a little jolt of something. Something that felt a lot like desire, which made no sense. He traveled too much to deal with complications in his relationships, and this woman was waving *complication* flags all over the place. He shrugged off that train of thought. "Look, I'm sorry I blew off your first text. I thought…"

"You thought I was crying wolf?" She was spot-on, but he hated to agree. It made him sound like such a jerk. He ran his fingers through his hair, shoving it away from his face.

"I'd had a bad week and a really long day. I reacted without thinking about what you were saying." He tried to soften his words with a smile. "And let's be fair—you *have* been a pain in my ass with your texts."

Her laughter bubbled up. "Sorry. And sorry again about tonight." She pushed herself to her feet. "I overreacted…"

"You *didn't*." He slowly stood, and the dog—

Sophie—started to growl, until Jillie reached down and touched her fingers to her head. He pulled out his flashlight, knowing it was going to be a tricky walk down the mountain in the shadow of the pines. "Don't ever hesitate to reach out. We should start down. Why were you climbing so high, anyway?"

"It was automatic. I love this old mountain, especially her craggy summit. In the summer I like to go up there and sit on the warm rocks."

"I don't think those rocks would be very warm tonight." The forecast had included a frost warning.

"I know. I wasn't thinking—I was in a panic. The rocks felt like they'd be…stronger than me."

He struggled to dismiss the effect her words had on his heart. She wanted strength. He wanted to provide it. But he wasn't a mountain. And he had a hunch that a man wasn't what she was looking for. A man was likely the reason she was in this state.

"Let's get down this trail before it gets any darker, okay? Are you more comfortable leading or following?"

He knew she was a nervous type. Her friends had refused to confirm it, but he was sure something had happened to her in the past. He didn't want to make any move that would trigger more fear. She thought about if for a moment, then nodded toward the trail.

"I'll follow."

The trail was steep up here, but relatively smooth. The pine needles and fallen leaves made it slippery, so they took it slow. After a few minutes of silence, he spoke over his shoulder.

"You asked if the kids were looking for Bryce and not someone else. Who else would they be looking for?"

She didn't answer right away, and he wondered if she would at all. A thought came to him and he stopped and looked back at her, surprised to find her only a few feet away.

"Are you in witness protection or something? Are you hiding from someone? You thought you'd been found out?" Jillie hesitated, and Sophie began her usual low growl at him. Clearly, the dog hated his guts but didn't want to leave her master's side long enough to devour him. He turned and started walking again. The path was less steep down here. "You know what? Forget I asked. It's none of my business." The police chief and her other friends had made that clear. He heard her footsteps behind him.

"After what you did tonight, I guess I owe you an answer. You protect your brother's whereabouts, so I assume I can trust you to protect mine?"

He waved his hand without looking back. "Of course, you can trust me. I give you my word. But honestly, you don't owe me anything, Jill."

"Don't call me that." Her voice flipped a switch, sharp and angry. "My name is Jillie."

"O-kay. Sorry. I thought it was a nickname."

"It's not. My name is Jillie Coleman."

He could see the lights from her place ahead through the trees. "Got it."

Her voice softened again. "It's also J.L. Cole."

He turned when they got to her yard, beside the tall, narrow A-frame. The deck on the front was at the top of a long flight of wooden stairs. On the side, presumably from a second-floor room, a smaller square deck jutted out from the sloping roofline that swept almost all the way to the ground. He turned her words over in his head, trying to understand what they meant. And why that second name was so familiar. His eyes went wide.

"Wait. The *author*? The guy who writes all those horror books? That's *you*?" With as many hours as he spent on planes traveling with Bryce, he'd become an avid reader of thrillers and the occasional horror novel. Particularly the creepy ones by Cole, whose "bad guys" always seemed so…normal. Until they very definitely *weren't*. He smiled. "Obviously not the *guy* at all. I've read all your stuff."

The motion-activated flood lights around the A-frame—and there were a lot of them—showed the touch of pink that rose in her cheeks.

"I've actually never claimed to be a guy, but a lot of people make that assumption. And that's okay. Female authors often have a hard time getting a foothold in the crime, horror and sci-fi end of publishing. There are successful ones, of course, but it's still a pretty tight boys' club within the bigger boys'

club of publishing in general." She gestured to Sophie to go up the stairs to the deck above them.
"And thanks for being a fan. The problem is some
fans get…weird. Especially toward female authors.
Especially in a genre like horror. They think they
know us. That they have some right to express their
opinions to us on our books and our characters, and
some of those opinions are creepier than my books
ever thought of being."

She didn't look at him as she spoke. She stared
down the mountain beyond the driveway where he'd
parked, or more like abandoned, his car after getting
her texts. Maybe he'd had her all wrong. Maybe she
wasn't a victim of anything more than a few obnoxious fans. Which was enough to make anyone paranoid and jumpy. Matt should know.

"I get it. With social media, people imagine themselves friends with celebrities just because their
comment got liked on some photo or video platform. They feel an intimacy that doesn't exist. It's
bad enough with Bryce being a sports star. People
want his autograph, and more than a few want to
climb in bed with him." And Bryce had been more
than willing to accommodate those requests over the
years. "I hired a bodyguard for Bryce for a while
after he won the gold medal. The guy told me it was
worse with actors and writers. Their fans imagined
themselves involved with *fictional* characters. They
weren't dealing with reality. He said it makes them

more unpredictable…" Matt's voice fell. "And I'm really not helping things right now by telling you that. Sorry."

She gave him a fleeting smile. "Nothing I didn't already know, Matt. I should get inside. Please…I'm trusting you with a secret very few people know."

"People like Dan Adams and your other friends in town?"

She nodded. "They know how to make me feel safe, you know?"

Matt was shocked at the power of the emotion that struck him at those words. He wasn't a violent man—he preferred negotiating his way out of problems. But in this instant he urgently wanted to beat the ever-loving daylights out of anyone who'd ever made Jillie feel *un*safe. He looked up at the security lights. There were probably cameras up there, too. He swallowed hard, not used to feeling so…so *much*.

"And your secluded mountainside home with the fancy electronics is part of that safety net? Along with your hellhound?"

Jillie chuckled, looking up to where Sophie was glaring down at Matt from the deck. "Don't insult my dog. She's more ther—companionship than protection. Although, her appearance doesn't hurt." She shuddered and pulled her jacket tighter.

God, he'd kept her standing out here in the cold and dark while he grilled her with questions.She'd already hinted that it was time for him to go. He scrubbed his hands down his face. He didn't want to leave her.

"I'm sorry, Jillie. You must be freezing. Go on up. Once I know you're inside, I'll take off."

"You were probably on your way to dinner. You must be starving." She hesitated for just a moment. In that moment he *really* wanted her to invite him up, but, of course, that didn't happen. Instead, she flashed him a quick smile before turning to go. "Thanks again, Matt."

Way too complicated. Just let her walk away.

She was on the deck before he called out to her.

"We've got the old ski lift working, but I need to give it a few test runs, to get acquainted with the thing. If you want a ride up to that rocky summit you like so much, I'll be heading up there Sunday afternoon. It'll just be us. No workers. No spectators."

Her head started to move back and forth, then stopped. She looked down at him in silence, then gave a loud sigh. "Maybe. I'll let you know. I've… I've got to go in."

He watched her and Sophie go through the door. She turned and locked it, then gave him a tentative wave. For someone obsessed with privacy, it was interesting that this entire wall, right up to the peak of the A-frame roof, was glass. He lifted his hand, then headed to his car. He wasn't sure what surprised him more. That he'd asked Jillie to ride to the top of the mountain with him, or that she'd said...maybe. As he turned the ignition, he realized he was smiling.

Chapter Five

*Robbie sat by the fire, staring into the dancing
flames that sent shadows across his troubled
face. It struck Monica that perhaps she wasn't
the only one with stories to tell. They'd all lost
something to the monsters of shadow. Maybe
she wasn't so alone after all.*

Jillie stepped out of the woods on Sunday afternoon,
glancing around for any activity before walking
across the grassy ski slope and down to the lodge.
She tried to tell herself this wasn't strange at all.
Just a woman with agoraphobia leaving her house,
and her property, to go somewhere she'd never been

before. Alone. To meet a man she barely knew. Perfectly normal.

Mack had been stunned into silence at the news over lunch yesterday. Jillie had met Mack, Nora and Amanda Randall at Amanda's home. It was no ordinary home. It was a historic castle named Halcyon, built well over a hundred years ago. And rumored to be haunted. Amanda was an interior designer, and had renovated the old place into a comfortable, wide-open family home a few years ago—just before Jillie moved here. And then Amanda married its owner, Blake Randall, and they'd started a family. Halcyon was one of Jillie's safe places to go, mostly because of its size—she never felt closed in there. And also because Amanda had become a dear and trusted friend.

"So let me get this straight," Mack finally said. "You heard a group of people on your property at night, and reached out to *Matt Danzer* instead of one of us, or calling Dan?"

"Well…that's not exactly how it happened." She explained how she'd texted Matt first because she thought it was his workers, and then things had escalated quickly. But her friend had a point. She could have dismissed Matt and called the police chief. She'd started to, but…then Matt was on his way to her. Coming to her rescue. Mack and Nora, Amanda's cousin, clucked their tongues and cautioned her to be careful. Amanda had remained silent.

Amanda pulled her aside after the lunch, as everyone was leaving. She'd experienced her own version of childhood trauma, being date-raped in high school. She understood Jillie's anxiety disorder on a level few could. Amanda had brushed her long blond hair over her shoulder before grabbing Jillie's hand.

"I know everyone's telling you to be careful, but let's face it—no one's as careful with their hearts as people like you and I." Amanda smiled. "So I'm going to tell you to…not be *too* careful. Careful can get lonely, as you well know. Trust your instincts, of course, but…if this Matt guy is igniting some kind of spark in you, don't be too quick to extinguish it. See where it takes you." She looked around the home she and her husband, Blake, had created for themselves. "Not all surprises are bad."

See where it takes you…

Where it had taken her on this bright November Sunday was out into the open, walking to the Gallant Lake Ski Lodge to meet Matt. She walked up to the lodge, which was larger than she'd expected. And in better condition. It looked like it had a fresh coat of paint, at least.

She wouldn't go so far as to say Matt made her feel *comfortable*, but…not terrible, either. Not panicked. Just…cautious. But hell, even *that* was an improvement over what she'd have felt with anyone else.

It wasn't as if she'd swooned at his square-jawed smile and twinkling blue eyes. His golden hair that always looked like he'd just raked his fingers through it. Jillie stopped, feeling an unfamiliar flush under her skin. She wasn't helping herself by cataloging all of his charms. Charms that had no effect on her at all, of course.

He stepped out of the lodge and onto the wide flagstone veranda above the parking lot, raising his hand to greet her. Even Mother Nature liked the man, as the wind ruffled his sunkissed hair.

"Do you want a tour of the lodge before we head up the mountain?"

Jillie blinked. His small SUV was the only car in the lot. But still…she and new places didn't get along, and just *being* here was a huge move for her. He turned to lock the door to the lodge, calling to her over his shoulder.

"Never mind. Maybe another time. I'm feeling proud of this old place, after thinking it needed a match set to it a month ago." He was being careful to stay on the far side of the steps as he came down. She wasn't sure what to make of the butterfly flutter she felt in her chest at the realization that he was doing that for her. He stopped a few feet away, leaving her plenty of personal space. Another flutter. He grinned. "I'm glad you came. To be honest, I was surprised to get your text earlier."

She didn't want to admit that she was surprised, too. "Getting up to the summit was a temptation I couldn't resist." He zipped his winter jacket and gave her a wide smile. *Wow.* The summit wasn't the only thing she couldn't resist. She cleared her throat. Twice. "Uh...the lodge looks sturdier than I expected, after being empty for so long."

He squinted up at the long, low building hugging the mountainside. "It was pretty rough when we got here. A *lot* rougher than I expected from the photos on the auction site." He patted the fieldstone wall. "But we got lucky, because the structure itself is solid as a rock. It was built to last, and just needed a little love and a lot of updating."

They walked around the building together, and he pointed proudly at each accomplishment. The new, energy-efficient windows. The fresh blue-gray stain on the cedar shake siding. The solar panels being installed on the roof. A new layer of crushed stone in the parking lot. A new heating and air-conditioning unit. A massive generator sitting on a cement pad behind the building. She'd had no idea so much work had been happening over here. The outdoor ski hut and snack bar above the lodge had been stained to match, and sported a new roof and bright yellow door and shutters. A wide swath of ground had been bulldozed and leveled nearby. He gestured toward it.

"We're expanding the outdoor dining area. The flagstone for that is arriving this week, so it will match the veranda. It will be partially covered, and we'll have propane heating towers to keep it as toasty as possible." He looked over to the opposite side of the slopes from her house. "And it should be popular in the summer, after people use the Alpine slide and the zip lines."

Her heart fell. "You're going to be open in the summer months, too?"

"We're going to fix up the old cement slide and add zip lines. People will be able to take the ski lift to the summit, then choose their way down. Or just take in the views from up there and ride the lift back to the lodge." He picked up on her displeasure at the idea. "Jillie, going year-round is the only way to make any profit with this place. Getting the right temperatures for good snow cover is a gamble with global warming and all that. If we have a warm winter, we won't make enough money to survive."

She didn't answer. The man had a right to make a living. But the thought of this place crawling with customers year-round sent a chill through her. People wandering into the woods. *Her* woods. Maybe she could talk him into building a fence. They continued around the buildings in silence for a few minutes.

"Why *Jillie*?" he asked out of the blue. "I mean, was that your birth name?"

If he was looking for a safe new topic, that definitely wasn't it. She swallowed hard, keeping her voice steady.

"My birth name was Jillian, but I don't use it."

Just like everything else her birth mother had given her, it was useless.

Matt hesitated, as if he wanted to ask more. He seemed to be simply curious.

"Jillian is a pretty name. What don't you like about it?"

There was something about the man that inspired blunt honesty in her.

"I had a foster mother who insisted on using my full name." They stopped at the base of the ski lift, which was also sporting a fresh coat of yellow paint. She broke eye contact, looking up the mountain. A hawk swooped between the treetops before disappearing from view. "The way she used it made me hate it."

He paused, digesting her words with a frown. "Okay. But why Jillie instead of Jill?"

Matt was trying to make small talk. He had no way of knowing how loaded his questions were. She did her best to give him a relaxed smile.

"You don't think Jillie suits me?"

"It doesn't exactly scream *I write horror novels*, but…" He tipped his head slightly. "Yeah, I guess it suits you just fine. But Jill is the more traditional variation, right?"

She stiffened, her eyes closing tight. She could feel Ted's hot breath across her skin in the darkness.

Don't make a sound, Jill. Stay quiet, Jill. Don't tell anyone, Jill.

"I told you not to call me that." Her voice was hard. There was a beat of silence before Matt spoke.

"You did. I'm sorry."

When her eyes finally opened, he was staring at her, but not in a way that made her uncomfortable. It was as if he was telling her with his calm, steady gaze that, as much as he might want to know more, he was done. The pressure in her chest eased a little, especially when he immediately took the conversation in a different direction.

"Do you ski at all?"

"I prefer cross-country skiing. It's a faster way to glide through the trees than snowshoeing, and the old trails are still pretty accessible for cross-country."

His brow arched. "You snowshoe? I never got the hang of it. Too much work."

"It's not hard once you get going, and it's the only way to get through fresh powder on the trails."

"I prefer my powder under a pair of skis, thanks."

"You like it the easy way—downhill and fast. Got it."

Matt's eyes darkened a shade.

"I don't like *all* things easy and fast, Jillie."

Was he *flirting* with her? She couldn't remember the last time a man actually flirted with her. Or maybe he was just being literal. But...it felt like flirting. He'd turned away rather abruptly, so she couldn't read his expression to make a determination. He headed toward the small hut near the lift, stepping inside the doorway to power it up. When he returned, he took another conversational detour.

"You can't see the slopes or lodge from your house, can you?"

"Not really. I can see the upper slope from my bedroom window, but not in the summertime." What was his point? "Even in the deep winter, there are enough evergreens that it's hard to see this far."

He ran both hands through his hair, then held them there, fingers intertwined on top of his head. He seemed lost in thought for a moment as he stared at her.

"I'm just sayin'... If you can't see the place, and if you haven't heard all the construction going on here at the lodge, then...maybe this place being open won't be as disruptive as you think it will."

"Maybe. But there's nothing stopping people from exploring those trees between us. Maybe you could put up a fence or something."

He didn't answer, but his expression said volumes when he looked past her toward her place. A fence would be a major undertaking. He flipped a large lever on the side of the shack, and the motor inside ground to life. The lift seats, hanging from the cables above, began moving slowly. He grabbed one and lifted the security bar so they could hop into the seat together. It was now or never. She took a deep breath and stepped on the platform, getting swept into the seat and up the slope with Matt at her side.

The ski lodge might not be as disruptive as she feared. The presence of Matt Danzer on her mountain, however, was proving to be very disruptive indeed.

The trip up the mountain was silent. Matt couldn't figure out if it was a tense or comfortable silence. The atmosphere on the lift seemed to careen between the two, although not a word was spoken. He might never figure out what was happening when he was around Jillie Coleman.

As they reached the summit, he made a mental note to talk to the guys about how jerky the cable was up near the top. The shudder wasn't enough to make the chair buck. It was just a vibration, really. He wanted to make sure it wasn't going to be a safety issue once the lift was loaded with skiers. When the chair started moving around the huge wheel at the summit, he reached for Jillie's arm, just to make sure she knew to hop off before it was too late and the chair swung out over the rocky drop-off to return down the mountain.

As usual, Jillie was ahead of him. She'd already

hopped off and moved to the side. He followed, shaking his head in wonder.

"I thought you said you didn't ski?"

"I didn't say I *never* skied. I said I prefer to do cross-country." She moved up the incline toward the rocky mountaintop while he hit the large red stop button on the lift. "To be fair, I haven't skied *much*. And it's been years."

"Because you're so nervous around people?" He muttered a curse under his breath. "Damn it. Sorry. I swear I know how to be tactful, but when I'm with you I…"

She looked over her shoulder at him.

"Lose your filter?"

He barked out a laugh. "Yeah. I don't have much of a filter, anyway, but with you? None at all."

He couldn't filter how much he wanted to know about her. For a guy who didn't hang around a place long enough for real relationships, it didn't make sense. He'd never met anyone like her, and he wanted to examine her like a specimen. No, that didn't sound good. He wanted to *know* her, damn it. And she wasn't making it easy.

She'd moved ahead, walking faster as she neared the old fire tower near the summit. "I haven't been up here since midsummer. I've only made it up here in the cold weather a few times. It's a treacherous climb if there's even a little bit of snow on the ground." She pointed down toward the town. "You can see a lot farther without the leaves on the trees. There's the resort. And Halcyon. See the castle?"

He recognized the resort because he and Bryce had been there for dinner a few times. But he hadn't seen the historic old castle before now. He'd heard about it, of course. Blake Randall and his family called it home. It was pretty impressive, even from way up here, with two round towers and the pinkish granite glowing in a shaft of sunlight that made the place look like a fairy-tale mirage on the lakeshore. Jillie was still smiling fondly.

"You've been there?" he asked.

"It's even prettier inside." She nodded. "Amanda Randall is an interior designer—she helped me redo my place a couple years ago."

"So you…you have more friends here than the liquor store lady and the coffee lady. You go places…"

She rested her hand on the rusty metal framework of the fire tower. "I'm not a troll living under a bridge, Matt. Of course I have friends. I go out sometimes." Her tone softened, losing its defensive edge. "My friends understand what I need. They go out of their way to make sure I feel safe."

She'd said that before. He couldn't wrap his head around all of her fears and how she managed them.

"What do they do?"

Her forehead creased in confusion.

"What?"

"What do your friends do to make you feel safe?"

The wind was stronger and colder up here, and a gust had both of them pulling their jackets tighter. They headed down toward the sparse and twisted tree line near the ski lift. The wind was coming from the west, behind the mountain, so it was just enough to get them out of the worst of it. Jillie moved to an outcropping of rocks, sitting on one that had been soaking up the sun for a while. Matt kept a few feet between them to make sure she was comfortable, leaning his hip against one of the larger boulders there and looking down to where she sat. She stared out over the valley, and he thought she was going to ignore his question entirely. When she did speak, she continued to look at the lake and that fanciful castle where her friend lived.

"It's more about what they *don't* do. They don't bring strangers around. They keep the number of people small enough that I can have my space. They let me know where all the exits are, and where I might be able to be alone for a minute if I need that. I know the floor plan of Halcyon and places like the coffee shop or the liquor store. They're almost as familiar to me as my home." She gave him a rueful smile. "Sounds silly, doesn't it?"

He shrugged. "It explains why I saw you go into the liquor store last week and never come back out. You used the back door, like you did at the coffee shop?"

Her eyes narrowed ever so slightly. "Please tell me you're not stalking me."

He raised his hands in innocence. "I swear. I'd stopped at the hardware store to order some supplies from Nate and saw you across the street. I figured maybe you were drinking your purchase in-store."

The corner of her mouth tipped upward. "I've been known to taste some wines with Mack Adams, but not last week." Her face grew thoughtful, then she nodded. "I remember that day. I was buying some cognac, and a bunch of noisy businessmen from the resort came in to stock their rooms with booze. I went out the back."

"With the cognac? Smooth move."

She rolled her eyes. "I'd be a fool to steal from the police chief's wife. Mack put it on my bill. I have accounts with the people I know, just in case something like that happens."

Matt couldn't help but admire the way she'd figured out how to cope with her fears. She'd made a life here in Gallant Lake, and, as secluded as her world was, it worked for her. He still had so many questions. None of them were any of his business, but as usual around her, they tumbled out anyway.

"You mentioned a foster mom before. You grew up in the system?" Her body tensed, and he kicked himself. "Sorry. I don't mean to pry, I just…"

"Just *what*, Matt? Do you pepper everyone you meet with questions like this?"

"Only the ones I care about."

He cleared his throat and tried to regain some self-composure. The only sound was the shushing of the wind through the pines around them, but the sun had warmed the stones enough that they weren't freezing. Or maybe it was the buzz of energy that always seemed to spin between them that was making his chest feel warm. Once again, he thought she might ignore his question, but he was beginning to realize Jillie needed time to think through her responses. As if speaking incorrectly frightened her almost as much as crowds did. Her shoulders lifted and fell with a deep breath.

"I was in foster care most of my childhood. My biological mother gave me up when I was five. She had better things to do, like drugs and booze." The childhood hurt resonated through her words, even though her voice was eerily level and matter-of-fact. "Some of the homes were okay. Some were…not."

He thought of her insistence that she not be called Jill or Jillian. Identities she'd had as a foster kid that she did *not* want to be reminded of. His fingers curled at the possible reasons behind that.

"Did you…were you…?" His voice trailed off. If ever there was time for him to *not* push her, this was it. A few minutes went by, but the silence between them was no longer comfortable. It was heavy with unasked questions and untold stories. An image came to mind, and it was one he rarely let tarry long.

It was Bryce as a scrawny ten-year-old boy, standing in the living room of their family home in Vail, pale and wide-eyed. A kid whose life had been turned upside down overnight. The thought of his brother being tossed into a foster-care system sent a chill down Matt's spine. Instead of asking questions, maybe it was time for him to tell Jillie his story. More than the glossed-over media kit version.

"Bryce was only ten when our parents died in a plane crash. Child services came knocking before their bodies were cold. They asked about other relatives and hinted they might take custody themselves." Jillie was watching him now, her eyes solemn and sad. "Mom was an only child, and Dad's sister had six kids of her own. She'd have taken Bryce if she had to, I suppose, but they lived on some ramshackle, off-the-grid homestead in Idaho. And her husband was an overbearing ass."

"How old were *you*?" She'd guessed how the story ended.

"Just turned twenty. I was starting my third year at Colorado State." A hawk screeched overhead as he angled his wings into the wind. "I dropped out to raise Bryce, but if I hadn't been there…"

"He could have ended up like me." She finished his sentence for him, then hesitated. "He was lucky to have you."

His mouth twisted into a half smile. "He doesn't always see it that way. He was hell on wheels as a teenager. Especially once he started winning competitions and thinking he was the big cheese." He sat on one of the rocks near her, stretching his legs out in front of him with a heavy sigh. "I made a promise, though."

"A promise? To Bryce?"

"To my parents." He could still feel the hot Colorado sun on his back as he stood beside their graves. "After they died, I went to the cemetery and I promised them I'd do right by Bryce. That I'd raise him. Protect him. Always." It was a weight that had been overwhelming at times. He stared at the ground, then tried to shake off the melancholy with a soft laugh. "He hasn't made it easy. We're not just here for him to heal up from his injury. We could have done that anywhere. As his manager, I had to get him away from the groupies who only want to be near him for the parties and press coverage. Being skiing's wild child when he was seventeen was one thing, but it's time for him to grow up."

The corner of her mouth lifted. "That sounds more like a big brother talking than a business manager. You thought an abandoned ski resort might be a good place to hide him from the snow bunny paparazzi?"

He nodded. "That was the main reason. I'm not looking to lose my shirt in this place or anything. We'll focus on bringing in the locals this winter, and improve the place over time until Bryce is back on the circuit and I can get it sold."

"And then what?"

"No idea. Bryce will start training for the US team again. I usually follow him around and flip a few properties near wherever he's training to cover the bills. Hopefully, he hasn't burned too many bridges and we can get some sponsors. If he can behave. I just want him to be happy, you know?"

"It's going to be hard for you to stop acting like a parent."

He scoffed. "No harder than it will be for *him* to stop acting like a child."

She leaned toward him, looking up into his eyes from her perch below where he was sitting. "Hmm… my money's on Bryce. You're a caregiver right to your core, Matt. Even when you're at your most obnoxious, you have a part of you that is always looking out for the other person."

It was disconcerting to have her come so close.

"When have I ever been obnoxious?"

She chuckled, sitting back again. He wished she'd stayed closer.

"When *haven't* you? Right back to our first meeting when you were up in a tree and still being bossy about whose property you were on."

"And what about you, brandishing that fire extinguisher–size canister of pepper spray?"

She brushed her dark hair back over her shoulder with a saucy grin. "That was me being sensible, not obnoxious." She waggled her eyebrows at him, making his breath hitch. "Now if I'd *used* it on you, that could have been obnoxious."

A gray cloud scuttled in front of the sun, making their rock-strewn seating area sharply colder. He looked up at the sky and stood, reaching for her hand. He didn't trust that old ski lift in a windstorm.

"We should get back down the mountain before the wind kicks up any higher and we end up walking down. Not to mention getting cold and wet."

Surprisingly, she accepted his hand, which threw him. Sure, he'd reached for her, but that was out of habit. *Jillie's* habit was to avoid physical contact. Yet, her hand, small and tentative, was now in his. He was thinking of other words to describe the sensation as he pulled her to her feet. Tender. Warm. Electric. Sexy. He was distracted, and she was even lighter than she looked. His tug brought her bouncing right into his chest. He steadied her with his other hand on her hip, and they froze. Her lips—full, welcoming, plump—parted in surprise. Her eyes—wide, golden, brilliant—stared up at him. Her hair, shining like silk. Her cheeks, pale with high spots of color.

He blinked. God, he was cataloging the woman. Turning himself into a thesaurus to describe her features. Memorizing each and every one of them. Her other hand had landed lightly on his chest. Was she frozen in terror or simply as confused as he was? He didn't know how long they stood like that, with Jillie not exactly *in* his arms, but not exactly *not* in his arms, either. Her hand was still in his. Her chest rose and fell slowly. Steadily. Meanwhile, his own chest was barely containing his own wildly flailing heart. Something had to give. He either had to kiss this woman, or he had to release her. And without knowing what she was thinking, the options narrowed to one.

"Jillie…" His voice cracked like some horny high school teen. He cleared his throat and stepped back. He released his hold on her hip, but couldn't make himself let go of her hand. "Uh…we were headed down…um…down the mountain." *Smooth, Danzer.* "Before it gets…"

"Before it gets any hotter up here?" Sassy Jillie had returned, and at a most interesting moment. She gently pulled her hand from his, patting his chest before turning away. "I think that's a good idea."

Chapter Six

"No!" Monica cried, pulling away from Robbie and staring at her friends in horror. "You can't fall for their tricks. The Shadows want us to believe there could be good in them, but it's a trap. Why can't you see that? You can never trust them!"

Jillie sat back in her office chair with a heavy sigh as two of her favorite people argued with each other on her monitor screen.

"I'm just saying we should let Jillie finish this book before telling her to start a new one." Nia, her personal assistant, brushed a mass of skinny pink braids over her shoulder and sipped from a mug that read *Careful or I'll Put You In My Book and Kill You*.

"Jillie is a professional," Lisa, her agent, argued. "She's capable of multitasking. And it's my *job* to be thinking about her future. You're free to focus on the present, okay?" Lisa looked directly into the camera—at Jillie. Thick dark hair tumbled around her face. "Are there any problems with the present I need to know about?"

"Oh, look—one of you remembered I was in this meeting, too." Jillie rolled her eyes, which only made Lisa and Nia laugh. The three of them had a virtual conference call every month to make sure they were on top of things when it came to Jillie's career. They were a team—Lisa in Portland and Nia in Bermuda. They were also dear, and bluntly honest, friends. So the business meetings often veered off course like this. "You know, the actual *writer*? And no, I don't think there are any issues with the draft. The story is taking an interesting twist, but that's not unusual. My characters tend to have minds of their own."

Nia frowned. "What kind of twist? Is that why you haven't sent me any chapters in two weeks?" Nia had started as one of Jillie's biggest fans when she released her debut book, then became a volunteer beta reader. Her observations were spot-on and trustworthy. Once Jillie saw how organized Nia was, as well as being deeply invested in the book world and all the various online platforms for readers, she'd hired her to handle day-to-day things like correspondence, social media, managing her calendar and reviewing Jillie's draft chapters. And Nia was right—Jillie hadn't shared any in a while. Maybe because she wasn't exactly sure where this book wanted to go.

Actually, she *was* sure where it *wanted* to go, but she didn't know if it should go there. Or why this final book of the Monsters in Shadow series felt… different. Maybe because Jillie was feeling different these days? Letting more people into her life, like Matt and Bryce?

The younger Danzer brother had called her to apologize for his so-called groupies bothering her the week before. He'd joked about having "stalker fans" without ever indicating he knew Jillie's writer alter ego. That meant Matt honored his promise to keep her secret, even from his brother. Was that why the heroine in her book, Monica, had suddenly been so determined to trust some of the fellow resistance fighters she'd been intentionally distancing herself from in the other two books? Real life might be affecting Jillie's fictional world, and she wasn't sure if that was a good thing or not.

"Earth to Jillie." Lisa interrupted her thoughts. "If you're going to whine about being ignored, you can't zone out when I ask a simple question. Do you have chapters ready? *Is* there something I need to know?"

"I've met someone."

Jillie grimaced to herself for blurting that out. Then she remembered she was on a video cam. She opened her eyes to find two identical expressions staring back at her side by side—eyes wide, brows raised and mouths open.

Nia spoke first. "*You* met someone. How?"

It was a fair question for an agoraphobe.

"He bought the old ski slope next door."

"So it's a *he*." Lisa looked thoughtful as she sipped what was probably her seventh cup of double espresso that day. "And you met how?"

"Sophie chased him up a tree."

"Perfect meet-cute!" Lisa laughed. "Wait…when you said your book's characters were adding a twist, did you mean…?"

Nia whistled softly. "A J.L. Cole romance?" She tipped her head. "I don't think your YA fans would hate that. Some horror purists might, but you could always use a different pen name…"

Lisa waved her hand back and forth, interrupting. "Let's put the brakes on writing romance just yet. Jillie, you're not denying any of this. Do you and this new neighbor of yours have some actual chemistry going on?"

Her mouth opened, then she hesitated. Is that what she felt about Matt? Chemistry? Wouldn't that mean *desire*? Was chemistry a good idea? No, it wasn't.

"Oh, hot damn," Nia muttered. "Look at those pink cheeks. I'm guessing the answer to the chemistry question is a yes."

"No!" Jillie protested, refusing to believe it. "Not *that* kind of chemistry. But he's…nice. I had a problem last week, and he…he came to the rescue." She paused, knowing this next bit of information would send her two friends right over the edge. "He invited me to ride the ski lift to the summit of the mountain. And I did it."

Two mouths fell open again in perfect unison.

"You…" Lisa's face scrunched up, as if trying to imagine it. "You sat on a ski lift with a guy you just met? And went up a mountain with him? Did anything else happen we should know about?"

"Well…we talked for a while." She looked everywhere but at the web camera. "He knows who I am."

"Okay, *that's* it." Nia raised her hands in disbelief. "Who are you and what did you do with the *real* Jillie Coleman?"

Lisa was less amused. "Jillie, you protect your identity more than any author I have, other than maybe the grade school teacher who writes erotica. You're my little J. D. Salinger. And you decided to tell a near-stranger what you do? You told him your pen name? Does he know where you live? Can you trust him?"

"He's my neighbor, so yes, he knows where I live.

He walked me home the other night. I didn't invite him inside or anything, but…"

"But you wanted to?" Nia asked.

"Probably not."

Lisa's brows furrowed. "I'm sorry, did you just say *probably*? As in *maybe*? You let him walk you home? Like right to your door? *You?* The one whose home is a bastion of privacy?"

Jillie felt tension rise in her chest. This conversation was veering into uncomfortable territory. Or was she just avoiding confronting her own feelings about Matt? She tried to redirect, straightening in her seat.

"Isn't this call supposed to be about *business*?"

Nia grinned, completely unfazed by Jillie's attempt to be stern. "Aren't *you* the one who suddenly announced you'd met someone?"

Hard to argue with the truth. "Fine, but I don't want to talk about it anymore, okay? It's not a big deal…"

"Oh, it is," Nia said firmly. Lisa nodded in agreement.

"But anyway…" She cleared her throat. "Maybe the change in direction the book is taking is influencing my outlook, or maybe this new neighbor is influencing my book, or maybe they have nothing to do with each other." She paused for a breath, glancing at the time. "Oh, look—our hour is up, ladies. Nia, I'll send you some chapters tonight. Lisa, I'll start working on ideas for the next series…" She gave a soft laugh. "As soon as I have any, that is."

Lisa pursed her lips. "You know, there's no reason we can't spin something off the Shadow series. The publisher has expressed interest in keeping this new world of yours in play. It's different—not exactly dystopian, not exactly sci-fi, not specifically YA, but appeals to YA readers…" Lisa shrugged. "You said you're adding characters, so add someone who earns their own book down the road." She winked. "Or two. Or three. Maybe instead of a movie deal, we'll go for a streaming series."

Jillie shook her head, but her mind started to spin. The familiar type of spin that was already going "here's a new shiny idea we can play with," like a kitten discovering a basket full of Ping-Pong balls.

"Now look what you've done," Nia groaned. "I can see it in her eyes—you lit the story fuse in that head of hers."

They ended their monthly call with more promises and a hard refusal to discuss her new friend with them any further. But she didn't miss Nia's words as they ended the meeting…*be careful.*

Within a few days, she'd fallen back into a productive routine. It had been raining much of the week, which made it easier to focus on the book. Monica and Robbie, the leader of the resistance group, kept insisting on spending more and more time together on the pages, and Jillie let them have their way for now. She had another six weeks to finish the first draft, and if it didn't work, she'd just have to put in longer hours on her revisions to fix it. Wouldn't be the first time she'd reconstructed a book during edits.

She envied authors who were hyper-organized plotters—writing detailed outlines, knowing exactly what was going to happen in every scene before they started typing. That had never been Jillie. She'd written her debut seven years ago as a pure *pantser*, flying by the seat of her pants with no idea where the book was going to end up. That wasn't sustainable once she started signing contracts and committing to deadlines, so now she was what authors referred to as a *plotser*—a hybrid writer with a loose plan and some idea where the book was going, but also with a willingness to follow interesting detours when they popped up.

She'd tried the same approach this week with Matt and his contractors. His texts were as regular as usual, but the tone was different. More friendly. Or maybe she was injecting what she wanted to see in his briefly worded messages. She, on the other hand, had intentionally changed her approach. She stopped looking for things to complain about. Even when the contractor had to make three trips Monday morning to deliver the new snowmaking machines. Bryce had called again to apologize for that one. He explained that Matt had lost track of what the crew was up to. He'd been working side by side with the contractors all week, coordinating the electricians, the plumbers and the installers to get the job done as fast as possible. There was snow in the forecast, so she understood the urgency. If it was cold enough to snow, it was cold enough to *make* snow, which meant they could create a base on the slopes.

By the end of the week, she was pretty proud of her newly minted knowledge of how ski resorts operated. A walk with Sophie the day before made it evident that Matt had chosen to install snow lances to make snow along most of the slopes, particularly on the slope closest to her property. She'd done an internet search and discovered they were slightly less productive, but were quieter and used less energy than the large snow cannons Matt had installed at the very top of the slopes.

Was it weird that she'd looked all that up? Not really—research came naturally to a writer. She'd only done it so she wouldn't be surprised by anything that happened next door. Not because she had any interest in Matt Danzer's business.

Her phone vibrated in her pocket as she was cleaning, so she turned off the vacuum to check it. The motion sensors had gone off on her driveway cameras. She wasn't expecting anyone, but she recognized Matt's small SUV. Why was he coming to the house? Had something happened? She looked around in alarm. She wasn't a fan of unexpected guests, and her friends knew enough to always give her a call or text before just showing up. At the same time, there was a little charge of excitement pulsing in her veins. Matt was here.

Her phone buzzed again. A text from Matt.

I'm in your driveway. I have something for you. I can leave it or do you want to come out or...?

She almost forgot that she didn't like surprises. And he'd given her options to make sure she felt comfortable. It gave her the same warm feeling she'd had when he sat on the cold ground up on the trail. Her fingers hovered above the screen. Should she ask him up? At the last minute she chickened out, picking the middle option instead.

I'll be right down.

"Matt?" Jillie was propping the door open with her hip, tugging on her down jacket. "What are you doing here?"

"I was…" He suddenly felt foolish, watching her step outside with a thick woolen cap on her head. She was more prepared for an early snow than he was. When he'd headed over here, it was cold rain, but now it was sloppy sleet, smacking onto the dead leaves on the ground like little water bombs. "I wanted to check on you. They say this storm could get bad tonight. And I have some good news."

She'd left the hound of the Baskervilles inside, thank God. Sophie was not happy about it, though, barking angrily through the glass until Jillie turned, snapped her fingers and pointed at the dog. Sophie's bottom plunked to the floor and she went silent, but the dog's expression was pure malevolence toward Matt. Jillie looked down the stairs at him with a puzzled expression.

"Yes. I know. What made you think you needed to check on me?"

"I stopped by to make sure the lodge was locked up after the crew finished staining the floors. Stopping here seemed like the neighborly thing to do." He was starting to babble now, so he took a breath and grinned up at her, holding a bottle of wine in the air. "And I wanted to tell you that the snowmaking machines are in and ready to go. That's almost a week ahead of schedule, so no more daily contractor runs on the access road. On *your* access road."

She started down the wooden stairs toward him. "That's good news…for both of us, right?"

"Definitely." Then he cautioned her. "That doesn't mean I won't need to use the road a few more times, but I'll do my best to limit…"

"Matt, it's okay. Just give me a heads-up first."

He nodded. "No surprises." Ironic, since she seemed to surprise him at every turn. The sleet morphed into almost-snow with the next gust of wind. The tall pines groaned as they swayed overhead. He blinked against the pellet-like precipitation hitting his face. "So you're sure you're ready for the storm?"

Jillie's forehead furrowed as she got to the base of the stairs.

"Why are you here?"

Because he couldn't go another day without seeing her? Because he needed to hear her voice? See her face? Make her smile?

He handed her the wine. "A little thank-you gesture for letting us lease the access road. And to celebrate our early finish." She stared at the bottle as if she'd never seen wine before, making him falter. "I…Mack told me this was your favorite…"

She blinked. "It is. I just…I'm surprised."

"In a good way or bad?"

She pursed her lips. "Good, I guess." She smiled softly, as if surprised, and took the bottle. "Thank you."

A wet glop of snow hit him in the eye, making him flinch. Her smile deepened. "You should get going, Matt. There's no need to worry about me handling a snowstorm. It's not my first winter on this mountain."

"I should have known you'd be ready for Mother Nature without my help."

She chuckled. "I do appreciate the concern, but

I have a generator. I have a plow guy on contract. I have a well-stocked pantry. Plenty of firewood. That's how I deal with things—by being Little Miss Prepared."

He wished she didn't have to anticipate every possible outcome just to feel okay, but he admired her for being able to do it. The snow pellets had turned to actual snow now. This storm was coming on fast. Tiny flakes swirled through the air, spinning in circles before finally making it to earth, where they were beginning to accumulate on the leaf-strewn ground.

"Okay, Miss Prepared, you have my number if you ever *do* need anything." He suddenly felt very awkward. He had no reason to stay, and he didn't want to make her stand outside in the snow while he tried to invent one. He raised his hand in a half wave and turned to head back down to the car. This was totally cool. He was just a Good Neighbor Sam doing the right thing and taking his leave. Everything was fine. Until his boot hit the snow-slicked leaves and he fell flat on his ass.

"Oh, my God!" Jillie cried out, but damn if she wasn't laughing. "Are you okay?" She set the wine bottle on the steps and slipped and slid her way toward him, but he was on his feet before she got there, feeling like a world-class idiot.

He waved her off. "I'm fine. Nothing hurt but my pride."

Her hand gripped his forearm, briefly suspending his ability to think. Her eyes sparkled with amusement.

"I shouldn't laugh, but that was...well...your feet were higher than your head for a second there." She leaned back and looked him up and down. "Are you sure you're okay?"

His jaw worked back and forth. He tried to look as stern as possible, all while ignoring the sensation of her touch through his jacket.

"That was karma getting back at me for thinking you needed any help from me." He nudged her to the gravel driveway, away from the slippery leaves. "No sense in both of us going down." He looked up at the sky, where the snowflakes were getting fatter and heavier by the minute. "You should get inside. I need to head home before the roads are as slick as those damn leaves."

The corners of her mouth kept turning in as she held in more laughter, bringing out her dimples. He groaned to himself. *Great.* As if he wasn't infatuated enough with the woman, now he'd discovered Jillie had *dimples.*

She turned when they reached the base of the stairs going up the deck. Sophie barked a few times at their approach, and now stood inside, glaring through the glass in Matt's direction.

"Your dog hates me."

The dimples deepened. "*Hate* is a strong word. She's protective of me. That's her job."

"Is she a therapy dog or a guard dog?"

"Yes." She didn't elaborate. Her smiles were coming more often, and each one felt like a little gift. She moved up one step so she was almost looking him straight in the eye. "Thanks for stopping, but you're right about needing to get home. The roads will be bad."

"You'll call me if you need anything?"

She nodded. He started to turn away, but her next words stopped him.

"Sunday was nice." Her cheeks went pink. *Damn.* Blushing *and* dimples. She was killing him here. She hesitated, and her forehead creased. "I don't use that word very often to describe something unexpected, but…it was nice. Thanks for the ride to the mountaintop."

"I enjoyed it, too. You're a good person to talk to, Jillie Coleman." She always managed to pull words out of him that he didn't expect to share.

Her smile deepened, reaching her golden-brown eyes and softening them. "Really? I'm not exactly known for my glittering conversation skills. Most writers aren't. That's why we write. It's a very solitary profession." She tipped her head slightly. "Maybe it's *you*, Matt. You bring me out of my shell."

The snowflakes were clumping on her knit hat.

He couldn't resist brushing them away directly over her forehead. She went still. Not stiff or tense. Just… quiet. His hand dropped to his side, but their gaze didn't break at all. Then she surprised him by reaching out and brushing snow off *his* head. Her fingers slid through his wet hair, and a jolt of electricity shot from those fingertips straight to his groin. Her eyes went wide and dark, as if she'd felt the same thing. Even more interesting, her fingers were still tangled in his hair.

The snow was getting heavier by the second. Fatter flakes and more of them, creating a hush in the clearing as if a bubble had closed over them. Her fingertips moved slowly, brushing his scalp. He was afraid to move. Afraid of breaking the moment. Her brows lowered in confusion. She looked up at her hand as if she wasn't quite sure what it was doing. Touching him. He closed his eyes, feeling like a thirteen-year-old boy getting his first surge of testosterone. He was going to embarrass himself if he didn't step away, but he couldn't move. The bubble was holding both of them.

Something brushed his mouth, and his eyes flew open. Jillie's face was right there, her eyes looking into his. Her lips…her *lips* were against his lips. Barely, but touching him. She stopped moving when his eyes opened, so he did what any smart man would do in this situation. He closed his eyes and let her explore without being watched. Her mouth was like a feather, sliding back and forth on his. He could feel her breathing against him. Pressing more firmly. More confidently. He did his best to play statue, but it was torture. His hand rose to rest on her waist, fisting into her jacket to hold her there. Her hand slid from his head to wrap around the back of his neck. *Sweet Jesus.*

It was a real kiss now, and he *had* to respond. A man could only take so much. He tugged her gently against him, and she sagged against his chest. His arm slid around her and he began to kiss her back. Slowly at first, still afraid she'd wake up to what she was doing and push him away.

The softest of sounds—a sigh? a moan?—rose from her throat, and her lips softened and parted for him. *Let her lead. Let her lead.* He held on to his self-control for dear life, taking things slow and easy. His whole body shuddered from the effort. Did she feel it? Her other arm wrapped around his neck. His grip tightened on her. *Not too fast. Don't move too fast.* He might have made it if she hadn't traced her tongue along his lower lip. His self-control dissolved like the snow on his skin.

He pulled her closer and kissed her. A *real* kiss. Deep. Hard. And she didn't pull away. Instead, she turned her head to give him better access. She pulled herself higher on her tiptoes and he saved her the trouble by lifting her into the air without breaking the kiss. He dropped one hand lower to cup her bottom and hold her against him. She made another one of those kitten-soft sounds of desire. *Whatever you need. Whatever you want.* He set her atop the porch rail and her leg curled around his thigh, pulling him in. *Yes, please.*

Had he thought of what it would be like to kiss Jillie? Sure. He'd not only thought about it. He'd *dreamed* about it. Nothing in his imagination ever came close to this. His body was on fire for her. His skin burned with his need. His heart pounded in his chest, strong and rock steady. And speaking of rocks, the bulge in his jeans was rock steady, too. A low growl rose from his chest, and he knew he had to stop. Had to slow down. Had to think this through. He groaned out loud as he pulled his mouth from hers. Unwilling to release her yet, he trailed kisses across her jaw and to the base of her neck. He took a ragged breath and lifted his head to look into her shining, if slightly unfocused, eyes.

"Jillie…what the hell was that?"

Chapter Seven

Monica charged up the mountainside, sword in hand. But it was dark. Far darker than a typical night. She was too close. She was inside the Shadows. She couldn't see the path. One step more, and the ground disappeared from beneath her feet. She was falling.

It was a fair question. And Jillie didn't have an answer. Matt pulled just far enough away for her to be able to gather at least part of her wits around her, thanks to the layers of clothing they'd somehow managed to keep on. A flush of panic began to rise inside her. She'd basically attacked the man.

He hadn't exactly fought her off, but she'd initiated this…this kiss. Her eyes fell shut. Oh, God, she'd just kissed Matt Danzer. And not some shy peck on the cheek, either. She'd taken hold of his thick, glorious hair, held him there and kissed him.

Even now, her arms were around his neck, and her leg…what the hell was her leg doing wrapped around his thigh? She pushed herself back, forgetting she was sitting on the railing. Matt grabbed her jacket and steadied her. Like you would hold a child by the jacket, without touching them. His eyes were dark with…concern? Was he feeling *sorry* for her? Was he afraid she was having some weird episode that caused her to attack him? She couldn't breathe. She'd made a fool of herself.

She shoved against his chest again, but he held her coat firmly, talking low and slow. As if she was some wild animal who'd been cornered.

"Easy, girl. Take a breath. You're okay."

"Okay?" Her voice cracked. "How can you say I'm okay when I just…attacked you? I'm such an idiot. I'm so sorry…"

Amusement replaced the worry in his eyes.

"Baby, you can attack me like that any time you want."

His soft laughter poked at her pride, but quelled a little of her panic. She smacked his shoulder. "It's not funny, damn it. I took advantage when you had your eyes closed. I just wanted to see…" Her voice faded.

"What did you want to see, Jillie?" His face was close to hers, his words gliding along her skin, making her lose track of her thoughts. She shook her head in answer, so he guessed. Accurately, as usual.

"Did you want to see if you had the courage to do it? Did you want to see what would happen if we kissed?" He hesitated. "Did you like it?"

Her lower abdomen melted into a pool of quivering jelly. His fingers released her jacket, and he slid his hand around her. Under the jacket. Under her sweater. Against her skin. *Oh, God...* She dropped her forehead against his shoulder as his fingers glided across her back. Back and forth. Her nerve endings pulsed against his fingertips. She made a strangled sound.

"I did."

His hand stopped, then started moving again as he realized what she'd said.

"You liked it?" She nodded against him. He was almost whispering now. "Me, too, baby. Me, too."

Her head snapped up and she looked at him in suspicion. Without a doubt it was the best kiss she'd ever experienced in her life, but...he was literally a man of the world. Surely, her awkward attempt at a kiss hadn't been anything special to him. As if reading her thoughts, he took her free hand and slid it down to cover a prominent bulge in his jeans. An unexpected surge of pride flared inside her.

"I did that?"

His smile made the sun-worn skin around his eyes crease. "You're *doing* that." He shook his head in regret. "And if you don't remove your hand, you're going to do it to the point of embarrassing me right here on your front steps."

He stepped back abruptly. "We need to stop before we...don't stop." He raised his hands to the top of his head and laced his fingers together to hold them there. "Jillie, that was...it was incredible. And unexpected." Her cheeks flushed hot, and he rushed to reassure her. "That's not a bad thing, babe. Seriously...not bad at all. But...you and me...going any further than a kiss..." He winked. "Even if it *was* a world-rocking kiss...we need to think about what happens next."

A gust of wind swirled snow between their faces, even though they were only a foot apart. Jillie nodded, her heart full of questions and doubts. She looked down and sighed.

"And you need to get home. We both keep saying that, but seriously. You're going to have a tricky drive."

"Hey..." Matt cupped her cheek with his hand, and she found herself leaning into it. He gave her a tender smile. "Just to be clear, I *really* want to kiss you again. But I don't want our bodies to decide what comes next—I think we know what *they* want." He winked. "I want to be sure our heads make that decision." He glanced up at the falling snow. "This has been the longest goodbye ever. I gotta go."

She was tempted to ask him to stay, but then what? She chewed her bottom lip. He was right—neither of them was thinking clearly at the moment. That kiss had jumbled her brain cells into a roaring bonfire of desire, which was a brand-new sensation for her. One she needed to spend some time examining.

"Like you said, we need to make sure we're thinking this through and not being impulsive." Because *impulsive* rarely worked for her. "Text me when you get home so I know you're not in a ditch somewhere."

His smile deepened, his gray-blue eyes warm and tender. He leaned forward, placed a soft kiss on her forehead and promised he'd text. She watched his car head down the drive, then went up the steps and inside, shedding her wet coat and hat. This would be a good night for a fire. She'd just lit kindling under some logs when Sophie let out a low growl at her side.

Sometimes dogs did things that weren't great for the nerves. Like those times when a dog stared intently at what seemed to be nothing outside a door or window, hackles rising on her back. And then growling at it. Was she seeing her own reflection in the glass? A ghost? A figment of doggy imagination? Jillie shook herself. No wonder she wrote horror novels with this overactive brain of hers. She stood and turned toward the window wall, and let out a quick squeak of fear when she saw a man-size shape reaching the top of the stairs and moving onto her deck.

Sophie charged forward, barking furiously. The noise made Jillie squeal again, but as she stared at the apparition, she recognized the general shape. The blue wool coat. The soaking-wet golden hair. *Matt?* Sophie was literally flinging herself at the glass now, her barks turning deeper and even more threatening. Jillie gave a sharp command. Sophie stopped barking, but her growl was low and continuous.

Matt stood on the far side of the deck, apparently nervous the Rottweiler might actually bust through the triple-pane glass to come after him. Jillie's heart was racing at the unexpected visitor, but…this was Matt. She hadn't heard an alert on her phone, but sometimes the driveway camera got covered with snow. She finally forced her feet to move and opened the door, pointing at Sophie sternly until the dog retired to her bed in the corner, still grumbling and growling.

"Matt?" She blinked at him through the blowing snow. "What are…?"

He brushed his hands on his thighs, and she noticed his pant legs were hanging wet and heavy against his skin.

"Did you fall down again?" She grinned, but he didn't return the smile. The wind gusted and she gestured for him to come in. "Get in here before you turn into a Popsicle."

His jaw was tight as he walked past, his eyes looking anywhere but directly at her. His cheeks were ruddy and red…was it the cold or was he *blushing*? He stopped just inside, looking down at the clothes she could now see were completely water soaked.

"I don't want to drip on your floor…" he started.

She waved him off. "Forget about that. That's why the entry is slate. Kick off your boots, though. I was starting a fire, so you can warm up there. What on earth happened?"

He slowly shrugged off his coat, his face turning an even deeper shade of red. "Remember when you warned me about ending up in a ditch somewhere?" He met her gaze. "Turns out *somewhere* was right at the end of the road. A gust of snow blinded me for a second, and I turned too short…and slid straight into the ditch."

The ditches at the bottom of the mountain were deep and wide, made that way to accommodate heavy spring runoffs. Large culverts crossed under the main road at intervals to send the water all the way down to the lake. She'd noticed when she got her mail that afternoon that the ditches were looking like whitewater rapids after a few days of heavy rain.

"Oh, my God. Are you hurt? Is your car okay? How did you get out without…?"

"Without drowning?" He grimaced a bit as he moved his shoulder in a circle, testing it. "It wasn't easy. The car was nose-down, and I was basically hanging from the seat belt." He rubbed his chest. "Once I got myself unbuckled, the steering wheel broke my fall nicely. I crawled out the passenger door and made a leap for the high side of the ditch. There was a little tree there that came in very handy. It kept the top half my body from being submerged in ice water."

"Go sit in that big chair while I get the fire going. There's a blanket…"

He shook his head. "I'm a muddy mess. And honestly, I'm chilled to the bone. What I'd really like first is a hot shower." Her brows shot up, and he gave the first hint of a smile. "Alone. I don't know what I'll do about clothes, but these pants feel like they're freezing directly to my skin…"

Jillie's pulse jumped. She was way out of her element here. A man she'd just kissed the daylights out of was standing in her house asking for a *shower*. She counted to herself, focusing on picturing the shapes of the numbers instead of her rising panic.

One, two, three, four…

Feeling a little more in control, she tried to work out a plan. Plans calmed her. But what plan was there for Matt Danzer naked under her roof? She blew out a forceful breath, knocking that vision straight out of her head.

"Okay. Of course." She splayed her hands firmly, palms down, as if calming a wild animal. Except that wild animal was her own imagination. She looked up with a bright smile, as if men showed up here all the time asking for showers. *This was fine.* "Use the spare bedroom, down the hall on the right. There's a shower in there. It's not big or fancy, but it will do the job. There are towels on the shelf above the toilet. As far as clothes..." She looked around, willing a rack of men's clothing to appear. Oh! Men's clothing! She almost laughed in relief. "I almost forgot—I was putting together a donation box for charity, and Cassie from the resort dropped some things off. I'm sure she had some of her husband Nick's clothes in there." She eyed his frame quickly. "They should fit. At least until we can get these washed and dried."

His shudder was so slight she almost missed it. From the clench of his jaw, she could tell he'd been struggling to hold it in. He had to be freezing. She grabbed his arm and pushed him forward.

"Get in there. Right past the kitchen. Are you sure you're not injured? Do we need to call someone?"

Matt shook his head sharply. "I don't think so. I'll know more after the shower." He took a few steps in his stocking feet, then looked up in surprise. "Are these floors heated?"

"It's nice, isn't it?" She smiled. "I had it added when I remodeled. Look, I was going to cook up some angel hair pasta and marinara sauce. Does that sound okay for dinner?"

His eyebrows rose. "You don't have to feed me…"

"Well, I have to feed myself, and you're not going anywhere with your car in the ditch, so it looks like you're here for a while. You may as well eat."

He looked past her to the snow falling outside, thicker by the minute.

"I guess you've got a point."

The steaming-hot shower helped Matt's mood somewhat, but this had still been a colossally bad evening. The rushing water in the ditch had chilled him to the freakin' bone. His car was wrecked. His shoulder was sore. He'd felt like a fool trudging back up the hill to Jillie's place, but where else was he going to go? His phone had tumbled into the black water, so calling for help wasn't an option. He braced his hands on the back of the small shower and dropped his head, closing his eyes.

The day hadn't been *all* bad. He'd secured another investor that morning in Albany. And Jillie had kissed him. He smiled and stretched in the steam. On second thought, this day had been pretty damn good. Stellar, as a matter of fact. He put his head under the shower spray and shook it, feeling his muscles loosen up at last.

That was some damn kiss. He literally hadn't seen it coming. It was one thing to have her lips touch his, but when she pressed up against him and let him kiss her back…wow. That was a fireworks-and-big-brass-band kind of kiss. She'd doubted herself after he'd pulled away, so he'd tried to reassure her. By putting her hand. On his erection. That was a moment, right there. Hot little Jillie smiling proudly with her hand cupping him. Why he hadn't gone off like a missile was a mystery. It was probably a contributing factor to why he'd driven his car—his *new* car—straight into an overflowing ditch. Did he wait there to flag down another driver to help? Nope. He'd walked right back up the mountain to get to Jillie.

He turned off the shower before he scalded himself. When he reached for a towel, he was surprised to see an unfamiliar pair of dark blue sweatpants and a…a pink-and-green checked dress shirt? His own clothes, including underwear, were gone. Which meant two things. He was going commando tonight. And Jillie had been in this tiny bathroom while he was naked in the shower. What would have happened if he'd turned around to see her standing there on the other side of the frosted shower door? *Had* she stood there? Maybe the steam had obliterated him completely. But what if it hadn't?

He pulled on the sweats, which were a little short. Other than that, they fit. The shirt fit, too, but made for quite the look with the pants. Being barefoot wasn't an issue with her heated floors. Even in here, he could feel the gentle warmth. Or was that because he'd been thinking of Jillie? He shook his head with a smile and opened the door. Where he was greeted by Sophie.

The dog's eyes were like lasers, watching his every move. A low, grumbling growl echoed in the hallway. Moving felt like a really bad idea. He cleared his throat and called out in a level tone, trying not to show the dog his fear.

"Uh… Jillie?"

"I'm draining the pasta," she called. "Do the clothes fit?"

"They'll do. But… I can't get out of here."

"Why not?"

"Your canine enforcer won't let me."

Being laughed at was not usually his favorite thing, but Jillie's laughter warmed him from the inside out. He heard the *swoosh* of pasta water going into the kitchen sink.

"Don't be ridiculous, Matt. Haven't you ever had a dog?"

"My parents had a beagle when I was a kid. He spent all his time charging off after rabbits in the woods behind our house." He avoided looking directly at Sophie. She wasn't growling at the moment, but her hackles were still up along her spine. "I never feared her eating me."

"Look Sophie straight in the eye, command her to sit and walk by her calmly…as if she was your non-man-eating beagle."

What were the odds of him making any *more* of a fool of himself than he already had tonight? He leveled a stern look at Sophie, and told her to sit. She looked surprised, but she did it, narrowing her eyes at him. Then he took a deep breath and walked past her. And lived.

He found Jillie in the kitchen. The dog followed silently. Jillie looked over the counter at Sophie.

"Good girl! Go to your place." Sophie gave him one last baleful look before going to the large dog bed in the corner. Jillie slid his bowl across the kitchen island. "We can eat by the fire. It will be roaring by the time we finish. Between the shower, the hot food and that shot of whiskey I put by your seat, you should be warming up in no time." Her lips twitched as she took in his ensemble. "You're cutting quite the California figure there, but it looks like it fits?"

He took the plate, loaded with pasta and delicious-smelling sauce. "The sweats are a little short, but they'll do." They sat on giant floor pillows in front of the fireplace, facing each other with their backs against two leather chairs. He grimaced at the sweats, which were even shorter now that he was sitting. "Why are *you* the one collecting for charity? I mean, you don't…"

"Go anywhere?" She finished his sentence. "I'm in charge of collecting, laundering and organizing. I can handle that much on my own, and it gives me a chance to contribute. Nora or someone will pick it all up when the rummage sale gets closer."

They ate in silence for a moment, other than the crackling of the fire. Something was gnawing at him though, and he couldn't help asking one more question.

"That doesn't bother you?" She looked up in surprise. "To have to do all those work-arounds to cope with…"

"With my agoraphobia? That's what it is, in case you hadn't guessed. And no, the work-arounds do the opposite of bothering me. I figure I can either live in fear of my next panic attack and have no life—" she shrugged "—or I can live my life in a way that lets me avoid panic situations and still *have* a life. It's my way of controlling something that doesn't want to be controlled."

They ate in silence again while he thought about that. It was ingenious, really, even if he couldn't ever see himself doing it.

"I was raised to fight things head-on rather than work around them, I guess." His head dropped back as he swore softly. "That sounded passive-aggressive as hell. Sorry." He shrugged at her. "I'm not saying I'm right, it's just my reality. But what you've done works for you really well, and I admire that."

Jillie sipped her wine and set the glass on the edge of the hearth. The fire had settled into a gentle flame, and the logs glowed in pulses of red heat. With the hot shower, the food, the fire and the beautiful woman sitting across from him…he'd almost forgotten about his dip in the icy ditch. Which no one else knew about. He grumbled a curse under his breath. *Bryce.*

"Damn. I forgot to call my brother after my shower. Do you mind if I use your phone?" Jillie shook her head, handing her phone to him, then using a slice of Italian bread to soak up the pasta sauce on her plate.

Bryce sounded agitated when he answered the call from Jillie's number. "Jillie, have you seen Matt by any chance?"

"Hey, Bryce. It's me."

"What the hell, Matt?" Bryce said something muffled, as if talking to someone in the house. "Yeah, it's him." Then his voice was clear—and angry—again. "The police chief is here, and he says they found your car in a ditch. Are you okay? Why are you using Jillie's phone?"

Matt grimaced. He should have called Bryce right away. "I'm fine. I'm at Jillie's. My phone's in the ditch along with the car. I walked up here and she helped me get warmed up…" Her eyes brightened with laughter at his choice of words, and his brother chuckled on the other end of the call, his anger forgotten.

"*Really?* Jillie Coleman warmed you up, huh? Interesting." Someone spoke in the background, presumably Dan Adams. Bryce responded, "Yeah, Dan, I'm surprised, too."

"I didn't mean it like that, you ass. She let me take a shower and…"

"You *showered* at her place? Well, this gets better and better!"

"Come on, Bryce. It's totally innocent." A spot of color appeared on Jillie's cheeks. That kiss hadn't been totally innocent, of course, but no one needed to know about that. After all, he and Jillie were both pretending to each other that it never happened. He cleared his throat. "Are the roads still lousy?"

"Dan says there are accidents everywhere. You should probably camp out with your totally innocent friend tonight." There was a muffled conversation on Bryce's end that Matt couldn't make out. "Dan said he's got a buddy with a body shop and he's got a tow truck. He can be there in the morning. So you and Jillie go have your pajama party." Bryce hesitated. "Don't do anything I wouldn't do…which, as you know, gives you lots of leeway, big brother."

Jillie had risen to take their bowls into the kitchen, so she missed Matt's rolled eyes. He ended the call with a succinct suggestion for what Bryce could do with his innuendo and advice, then set the phone on the side table. There was a photo there of Jillie graduating college. An older woman stood next to her, and they were both smiling brightly. There were other graduates milling around in the background. There was another photo of a young Jillie laughing with a group of women on a beach somewhere, holding a fruity drink in her hand. There was Jillie on horseback as a teen, smiling shyly into the camera.

She returned with a bottle of wine, a glass for him and a small plate of brownies. She sat cross-legged on the floor, and patted the pillow for Sophie to come join her. The dog did as asked, but not without casting him another suspicious look as she walked by.

"I'm assuming Bryce suggested you stay here for the night?"

He nodded. "Dan was there. He said the roads are awful. I can walk over to the lodge and sleep there…"

"Didn't you say they just did the floors? That won't work."

Her phone chirped, and she chuckled when she looked at it.

"That didn't take long. Dan's already let his wife know you're here." She held up the phone. "Mack wants to know if I'm okay."

"And are you?"

"Yeah. I'm fine." She tapped on the phone. "I'm telling her not to worry." She frowned at the screen.

"She's echoing what Dan told Bryce. The roads are terrible." She typed an answer while still talking to Matt. "Dan's going to have a busy night. You've already seen where the guest room is. Just stay."

She sounded at ease about it, which was another piece of the Jillie puzzle that didn't fit. She was agoraphobic. He thought that meant never leaving the house. And she just suggested he stay, as if overnight guests stopped by all the time. He was pretty sure they didn't. He gestured toward the pictures.

"You weren't always like this, were you? I mean… you didn't always have to work around your…um… fears…"

She stared at the photos, scratching the dog's head absently. "It's not *fear*, Matt. It's a phobia. I'm not scared, I'm phobic. Scared is what I feel when I see a big spider. A spider makes me jump or yell, and might even make my skin crawl, but it doesn't render me catatonic. Fear is an emotion. Phobia is a condition." She stopped, the corner of her mouth lifting slightly. "Sorry for the lecture."

"I can't say I understand the difference completely, but that makes sense." He glanced at the pictures again. "In these photos…"

"I've had anxiety most of my life, but my phobia didn't develop in earnest until I was twenty-five. I had an…episode…in Philadelphia." She stared at the floor between them, and he sensed she was sliding back in time. "I saw someone. Someone I never wanted or expected to see again. Someone I thought was in my past. And then there he was, in my favorite bar, right in front of me. Smiling. I couldn't breathe. I fainted. My friends called an ambulance. It was humiliating." Her voice dropped so low he could barely hear her. "I thought it would be a one-time thing, but then… I kept thinking I saw him everywhere I went. Worried about seeing him every time I left my apartment. Terrified that I'd look up in the grocery store with nowhere to turn and he'd be there."

Jillie closed her eyes and took a slow breath. He wanted to stop her, but he had a feeling she was lost in her own world right now and he didn't want to startle or disturb her. So he waited. He was clenching his wineglass so tightly that he had to set it down, afraid the stem would snap.

"I stayed home more and more. And if I did venture out, I *always* thought I saw him, so I stayed home again, and…" She looked up at him. "It snowballed into this." She gestured toward herself, and then the photos. "Instead of that."

"Isn't there a way to get help for it?"

She nodded, sipping her wine. "I've been in and out of therapy most of my adult life. They say the best way to treat this is a mix of medication and cognitive therapy, which is basically exposing myself to what scares me in small bites, then increasing it." She sighed, staring into the fire. "And I don't want to do it. I don't want to deal with changing medications and disrupting my writing. I've figured out a way to live my life and have friends. I mean, I'm okay, right?" She glanced at him and away again quickly, color rising on her cheeks. "I've even kissed a guy."

"Yeah, you did. You did a great job of it, too." He frowned. "I take it it's been a while…?"

Her color deepened. "A very long time. I was in a casual relationship when this all started. Kyle and I were basically friends with occasional benefits. My world started shrinking, which didn't leave him a lot of room." She stopped. Her brows lowered. Her voice dropped. "There was a time…before that… when I was in college…well…" She looked at him, her eyes troubled. "Let's just say you were far from my first kiss, Matt. I had a couple of wild years back then. I was acting out. Irresponsible."

He chuckled softly. "I've sown a few wild oats, too. That's part of life."

She nodded absently, only half hearing him. "By the time I moved to Gallant Lake, I'd been off the market for a good long while." A smile teased her lips, making him feel better. "Besides, the few men I've met here were either married to or engaged to my girlfriends."

"How did you get to Gallant Lake from Philly?" He stopped, waving his hand. "Never mind. You accused me on the mountain of interrogating you, and I'm doing it again, aren't I?"

She took another sip of wine, staring at him over the rim of her glass. She leaned against the big leather chair behind her, smiling down at a now-sleeping Sophie before meeting his gaze again.

"It doesn't feel like you're demanding answers from me. It feels like you...*care*."

Oh, he cared, all right. He cared a hell of a lot more than he wanted to admit—to her or himself. He kept his expression as neutral as possible.

"I do care, but I don't want to press you if you're uncomfortable."

She looked out the wall of windows, where the wet snow was still coming down. He could hear frozen sleet mixed in, clicking against the glass. Which brought up another curious question.

"Don't you feel exposed with all that glass? I know you didn't have neighbors before me, but still...that's quite a window."

She flashed him a grin, then called out a command. "Alexa, close all blinds."

A white cylinder on a side table glowed in response, answering her in a friendly robotic voice, "Closing all blinds."

There was a soft whirring sound and like magic, the copper-colored blinds he'd barely noticed before closed automatically. Instead of a nighttime snowstorm, there was a solid wall of warm color. And complete privacy.

His brow lifted. "Fancy." He looked around the

cozy A-frame. "You're not exactly roughing it up here, are you?"

Jillie shrugged. "I'm a recluse, not a hermit. I make a decent living from my books. It's not writers-in-the-movies money, with their martini lunches every other day and seven-figure advances, but I've been fortunate."

"*Fortunate* is buying a winning lottery ticket. You are *talented*, and you're being appropriately compensated for that talent."

She reached for the fireplace tongs and pushed a crumbling log to the back, making room for another. Matt pushed himself up to his knees and put the fresh log in. Once she'd closed the metal curtain across the hearth to contain the embers, she sat back down. Instead of sitting opposite him, she scooched close to his side, so they were leaning against the same chair.

Matt wasn't sure how to respond. Should he put his arm around her? Or give her her space and let her run the show, like he did with the kiss? She seemed to be struggling with what to do next, too, so he reached down and took her hand. Her fingers quickly intertwined with his, gripping tightly. He raised her hand to his lips and kissed her knuckles.

"This is nice," he whispered.

Her eyes were wide and dark. "It is." Her mouth quirked into a shy smile. "And thanks for the compliment on my writing. My agent will tell you I don't always know how to respond to that stuff. But I appreciate it." She leaned her head against his shoulder and they sat there, legs extended, entwined hands resting on his thigh, watching the flames begin to snap around the new log.

Matt tried to remember the last time he'd just held a girl's hand like this. Maybe high school? He sure didn't remember it feeling like this—relaxed. Intimate. Perfect. She rubbed her head on his shoulder and moved closer. *Yes, please.*

"And speaking of my agent, she's the one who suggested Gallant Lake. Lisa stayed at the resort for a conference, and said the town felt like it would be perfect for me. Not *too* remote, but definitely a ways from Philadelphia. I looked it up online, found a real estate agent and ended up here."

"Away from him." Matt didn't want to bring the specter of whoever had hurt her into the moment, but…there were so many unanswered questions. She stilled for a moment before nodding against him.

"Yes. My home city became impossible once I knew he was still there, too. As a writer, I can work from anywhere as long as I have Wi-Fi and coffee, so this was perfect. When I got my next advance, I gave most of it to Amanda Randall to redo the place. That's when it became a so-called *smart house*, with climate control, the automated blinds and a primo security system."

They sat in silence again. She'd changed the sub-

ject away from the mysterious *him*, and Matt was
okay with that. He leaned over and kissed the top of
her head, just because it felt like the natural thing to
do. He'd always been more of a cocktails in a hotel
room kind of guy. He and his dates always knew
where the night was headed. He had no freaking
clue where he and Jillie were headed. And he didn't
care. He kept his lips pressed against her hair. What
was this woman doing to him?

"He was in the same foster home as me."

Her words were dropped as casually as if she
was saying *the chair is blue.* Matt wasn't even sure
at first *what* she'd said. When the potential meaning became clear, the chill turned him colder than
when he'd waded through the icy water in the ditch.

"This guy was your foster brother?"

She went rigid, then shook her head sharply. "He
never did anything to deserve the title *brother.*"

"Got it." He squeezed her hand. "You don't need
to…"

"I was thirteen."

God damn. He didn't want to hear this, but she
seemed to need to say it. He released her hand, sliding his arm over her shoulders to pull her closer to
his side. Her eyes stayed fixed on the flames, but
she pressed up warm against him.

"It was one of those foster homes that churned
kids through like a factory, just to collect the checks.
He was seventeen and getting ready to age out of

the program in a few months. It started with typical pick-on-the-new-kid bullying. Insults. Shoving and tripping. Then…" She hesitated. "Ted came into my room one night. I think he just intended to scare me, but…he touched me and something changed in his eyes. When I started to cry, he told me to shut up or he'd…" Her whole body seemed to fall in on itself. Matt's heart clenched when she continued. "Or he'd hurt one of the younger kids. There were twins sleeping in the next room. They were nine."

Jillie went quiet. Matt combed his fingers through her hair slowly from scalp to tip. Sophie had shifted so her head was next to Jillie's leg, and Jillie's fingers tangled in the fur of the dog's thick neck. He cleared his throat, or at least he tried. Emotions had knotted everything together inside him.

"More than once?"

"On and off for months. There was no real pattern to it. He said if I told anyone, he'd hurt the twins. And I knew he'd do it." So she'd sacrificed herself. Over and over. At thirteen. He'd never consider Jillie Coleman afraid again. She was the bravest person he'd ever met. "So what happened to end it?" *Please tell me someone ended it.*

"The foster dad, or whatever you want to call him, caught Ted leaving my room one night. The school had contacted them because my grades were tanking and I kept falling asleep in class. I couldn't sleep at home, because I was listening to every little sound to see if he was coming. The fact that the guy suspected what was happening right away tells me I probably wasn't the first. I think the only reason the fosters reported him was because Ted was about to turn eighteen, so they wouldn't be getting checks anymore."

"Bastards," Matt muttered. "It was their job to protect you."

"Yup." She sighed. "Social services moved me and the twins. For the first time in my life, I got lucky. I lived with Sandy Ryan until I aged out, and even after that. She was old enough to be my grandmother, but Sandy was the closest to a mom I'd ever known. She's the one who started calling me Jillie, and helped me find who I was meant to be. She encouraged me to journal, and that's how the writing got started."

He felt the tension pulsing through her body begin to ease as she talked about Sandy. She looked up with a soft smile. "She was my biggest fan when I decided to write fiction. She told me to put my monsters on paper, and that's what I did. She lived long enough to see my first book published."

"So that's why you write horror? To exorcise your monsters?"

"I hope it helps other people exorcise theirs, too. In my books, women and girls are the heroes. That doesn't mean I paint all men as evil or anything, but my female characters tend to find a way to be the champion. I want girls to see themselves as having power."

"And *your* monster? Did they arrest him?"

"No. The system wanted the whole thing to go away. Nothing to see here, folks. They said they couldn't prove anything unless I wanted to testify, and even then, it was my word against his. I didn't want to go to court. I didn't want to sit there and tell people what he did. I didn't ever want to look at his face again." She shuddered. "So everyone just… moved on."

"You never had closure." He kissed her hair. "No wonder it's still messing with your head."

She gave a soft chuckle. "Thank you, Doctor Danzer."

"I'm sorry you lost Sandy."

"Me, too. She was in her sixties when she took me in, but it was still way too soon and way too fast. She had a heart attack. I never even got to say goodbye."

"I used to say that about my parents, too. I never said goodbye. But I think with the people we love, that's a moot point. They already know we love them. That we want them to stay here with us forever. They *know* we don't want to lose them. A spoken goodbye doesn't change that connection."

She pushed back and looked up at him, her dark eyes warm and just a bit amused.

"That's pretty deep, Matt." Her smile faded. "You became a parent to Bryce at a young age."

"I was twenty. I had to grow up fast, but I was ready. I had to be."

"You had to give up a lot."

Matt shifted as the latest log on the fire fell into two pieces, sending sparks and embers up the chimney. After hearing *her* story, it felt weird to think of what were basically inconveniences by comparison.

"I gave up…plans. Things that weren't real in the first place. It's not like…"

They both paused, and she broke the silence first.

"I hear you. I lost my childhood. And a big chunk of my emotional well-being. But you lost something, too. You gave up your future—at least, the future you'd envisioned." She looked up again. "What were you going to school for?"

"Architectural engineering." He gave her a slanted grin. "So I didn't give up that much. I wanted to design and build *new* things. Now I use that knowledge to rebuild *old* things, and that works fine. I started as a grunt with a friend of the family who was a contractor. Moe taught me everything about quality construction. No cutting corners. No saving a penny here when it might cost you a fortune to repair down the road. He offered to loan me the seed money to start my own company, but once Bryce got hot on the competitive ski circuit, we hit the road. I'd pick up a few houses or businesses to flip wherever he ended up training. Footloose and fancy-free."

"Do you miss having roots?"

"Nah. Bryce is a royal pain in my ass a lot of the time, but we're closer than a lot of brothers because of the life we lived. I wouldn't trade that for picket fences and a minivan somewhere."

"But Bryce is a full-grown man these days. You're not going to follow him around forever, are you? Because that would go from sweet to creepy pretty fast."

He snorted, but she wasn't wrong. Bryce had been pushing back at the idea of Matt continuing as his manager lately. But Matt liked knowing what the finances were and who Bryce was hanging out with. His vow to his parents was never far from his mind. There was bound to be a battle if Bryce got serious about breaking free.

He didn't want to think about that right now—or talk about it—so he tipped Jillie's chin up with his fingers, catching her by surprise. He lowered his face close to hers.

"Would it be weird if I kissed you right now?"

Her smile deepened. "Not at all. In fact, I think it would be very sweet."

And it *was* sweet. At first. Within mere seconds of their lips connecting, things got spicy. The kiss deepened, and Matt's arms encircled her, pulling her close against him. She turned, her leg sliding over his. His mouth never left hers as their bodies slid to the floor. She let out a soft moan, her fingers twisting in his shirt. His hands began to move, sliding down her sides, lining her up beneath him until he was settled between her legs. They were fully clothed as they moved against each other…and it was sexier than any other moment Matt could remember.

His fingers moved beneath her butt and gripped tightly as he slid back and forth. He didn't have to lift her hips—she was doing that on her own. She made soft little sounds as she turned her head to take the kiss to the next level. This kiss was sweet, all right. It was like sugar injected right into his veins—a sugar high he didn't ever want to end. He was still commando in these borrowed sweatpants. She had to feel him. Had to know he wanted to be inside her.

The thought made him dizzy. He'd never considered making love to this woman…well, other than in his dreams, which he had no control over. But right now? Right now it was the only thing in the world he wanted. Take the ski lodge, God. Take my car. Take my savings. Take it all. Just let me lie with Jillie Coleman tonight. One night. One perfect night.

He lifted his head, staring down into her wide, dark eyes. Her chest was quickly moving up and down. He placed his hand in the center of her chest, sucking in a sharp breath as he felt the frantic rhythm of her heartbeat. He took her hand and placed it over his heart. Her eyes went nearly black with desire.

"Do you feel that, Jillie? Do you feel how our

hearts are racing in the same damn rhythm? Like a team of matched horses?" He cupped the side of her face. "Don't we owe our hearts a chance to see what happens next? Can you imagine what it would be like to race together?" He kissed her soft lips. "I *can't* imagine it, but damn, I want to see it. Don't you?"

Her lips parted, her nostrils flaring, moving with each intake of air. Her eyes told a different story, though. Doubt and fear were taking hold.

"I do, but…"

He opened his mouth, wanting to scream *no buts!* That would make him a selfish SOB, though. And that was not who he wanted to be with Jillie. He closed his eyes and tried to harness his desire. Put the brakes on his plans. He wasn't going to pressure her, especially after knowing her story. He finally managed to nod his head, meeting her eyes again. Her hand was still over his heart, so he took it and lifted it to his mouth, kissing her palm.

"It's okay. I get it. We don't go any further unless you want to. I didn't mean to push you past what you're ready for." He started to sit up, willing his body to *stand down, trooper.* He held her hand, bringing her up with him.

Her mouth curved into a frown. She stared at him through thick lashes. The brave, sultry woman she'd just been started to fade away. Her mouth opened as if she was going to speak, then closed again.

"Hey…" He squeezed her hand. "Don't do that. Don't disappear. You know you're safe with me, right?" Jillie's head jerked in a shaky nod.

"Of course. I want to do more, but…" She chewed on her lip. "The panic attacks are *so* bad. What you saw on the mountain was *nothing*. Once it starts it's like a rolling cascade that builds out of control… And it is *not* sexy. I'm sorry, Matt."

He chuckled softly. "For what? Giving me some of the hottest kisses I can remember? Not to mention giving me the hardest erection of my life?" Her mouth twitched at that. "Tonight…hell, *today*…has been entirely unexpected. For both of us. It's okay to step back and think about things." Even if he didn't want to. "But it is *not* okay to apologize for anything."

He released her hand and started to slide away, putting some distance between them. But she stopped him, her voice low and shaky.

"Matt?"

"Yeah?"

"Just because we aren't going further doesn't mean…it doesn't mean we have to stop what we were doing…"

Matt willed his heart to remain steady. Could he keep kissing her tonight without wanting more? No. But he could kiss her tonight and not *do* more. He was a grown man, damn it. And if she wanted to keep this up, he was happy to oblige.

His mouth found hers and they started back at the beginning. It was sweet and tender, then grew from there. There wasn't as much raw fire as before, and that somehow made it…better. This was more controlled, more intentional. They weren't holding back, but they were both completely *committed* to every movement they made. Their heads tipped at the same time. Their tongues tangled and teased together. Their breaths were slower and deeper. They leaned in at the same time, and he reached for her waist at the exact moment she moved to straddle his hips. It was a dance—one they hadn't practiced, yet they knew every move before it happened.

Instead of imagining the end game, he let himself get lost in what was happening right now, in this very moment. Every touch. Every heartbeat. Every sigh. A random thought meandered through the back of his mind, whispering that this was very, very different. This wasn't just a kiss. This was him falling for Jillie Coleman. Not just wanting her in the physical sense, but…wanting her in *every* way. Wanting to know her. Wanting to please her. Wanting to feel her wiggle in his lap the way she was doing right now, which was the sweetest and most agonizing torture. The kind of torture he'd like a lifetime of.

Whoa. He wasn't a *lifetime* kind of guy. He barely knew this woman. And yet, it felt like he'd known her forever. Another word he didn't do. What the hell was she doing to him?

Jillie lifted her head, breaking the kiss and sending him even more off balance. Her dark hair fell forward, sweeping across his skin like a hot match. She looked deep into his eyes, then frowned.

"What's wrong?"

He kicked his doubts to the curb. He didn't know what was happening, but that was a problem for another day. Right now he wanted his lips back on hers.

"Not a thing, babe. Not a damn thing."

Chapter Eight

*"Why are you stopping?" Robbie demanded.
"Why are you being so cautious all of a sudden?"
How could Monica explain it? He didn't
know about the vision she'd had. The dream
of falling, falling, falling into the unknown. For
the first time in her life, Monica was afraid.*

Jillie stared up at the ceiling above her bed. She'd
said good-night to Matt just before midnight. She
could still feel the adrenaline surging through her
veins an hour later. Even if she could fall asleep,
she'd relive it all again in her dreams. Which wasn't

necessarily a bad thing, but right now she needed to think clearly.

It was one thing to kiss Matt on the steps outside earlier. That was impulsive. Playful…until it wasn't. She knew Matt had started that kiss in front of the fireplace to distract her from the stories she'd told him. He probably hadn't anticipated things getting out of control any more than she had. And he'd slowed down the minute he sensed her hesitating. She smiled up at the dark ceiling. Slowing down definitely hadn't been an easy thing for him to do. She'd felt him rock hard against her. If she'd given the nod, he'd have made love to her right there on the living room floor.

It wasn't that she didn't want that—every cell in her body was screaming with desire for him. He thought she'd stopped out of some sense of trauma from her childhood. There were other micro-traumas after that he hadn't heard about yet. Years of bad decisions when it came to men. It would be smarter to *not* do more than kiss. Doing more would be… messy. Unwise. Foolish. Dangerous.

But *damn*, that man could kiss.

And for the first time in years, she wanted… more. She closed her eyes, imagining Matt's hands on her again, but without any of those pesky clothes in the way this time. A soft sigh escaped her lips. Yeah, that was a very nice image. She could almost feel him touching her. Her hand flattened on her own stomach, and she pulled in a long, slow breath. It was good to know she could still feel like a whole woman. A desirable woman. It felt like a little piece of herself falling back into place.

She woke to the sound of shattering glass from the kitchen downstairs. Sophie leaped to her feet and stood at the top of the staircase barking loudly, her hair standing on end.

"Damn it!" Matt's voice was gravelly and low. "Ouch...shush, dog!"

"What's going on down there?" Jillie called out, reaching for her robe. She looked outside the glass doors to her balcony. It was still snowing, but no-where near as heavily as last night. The pale gray light told her it was shortly after sunrise. "Are you okay?"

"Sorry. I thought I could find what I needed to start cooking without the light on, but I knocked a wineglass into the sink." He hesitated. "Where *is* the light switch in here?"

Jillie could have told him, but instead she grabbed her phone. She opened the smart house app and activated the downstairs lights, then opened the blinds remotely, too. "Hang on, I'll be right down."

"Stay in bed, Miss Show-off. It'll take me a while to clean up and make breakfast. Unless you have some sort of cleaning robot you can activate from up there, too."

She slid her slippers on, debating whether she

should use the app to start the robotic vacuum, but that would be mean. "My cleaning robot doesn't like to share the kitchen." That much was true. Jillie swore that vacuum stalked her around the house, trying to trip her up. "What are you cooking? Can you find everything?"

"Looks like you have all the ingredients for my famous sausage-and-cheese frittata."

"Sounds delicious." She looked down at her robe, then took it back off. No need to get *too* familiar. She tugged on a pair of black leggings and a long, oversize sweater Nia had sent her for Christmas last year. It was the color of hot cocoa, and indeed had an outline of a huge mug of cocoa knit onto the front, complete with marshmallows made of fluffy white wool. She slipped on a pair of black canvas flats and headed downstairs.

Sophie followed, and they both stopped at the sight of Matt in the kitchen. A shirtless Matt. *My, my, my.* He'd surely heard them but hadn't turned. Instead, he was rapidly beating the eggs in a bowl. A frying pan was warming on the stove, with a pat of butter quickly melting in it. Jillie took a careful breath before trusting her voice.

"You look like you know your way around a kitchen."

He tossed her a quick grin over his shoulder, then poured the egg mixture into the sizzling pan. "I had no choice after becoming a quasi-parent at twenty. Bryce would have been happy with fast food every day, but he was a child athlete, so I had to up my game." He glanced down at Sophie. "She's not growling."

Jillie took the dog to the back door, answering over her shoulder. "She's preoccupied with an urgent need to get outside to do her business." She let Sophie into the fenced yard, apologizing to her for not walking her right away.

Matt poured the egg mixture into the sizzling pan when she came back to the kitchen, then gave her a quizzical sideways glance.

"Did you just *apologize* to your dog?"

She laughed as she poured fresh beans into the coffeemaker. "It would be rude not to, right?" After adding water and pressing the start switch, she turned back to him. She had to raise her voice to be heard over the coffee grinder. "You asked about her before—if she was a therapy or guard dog. She's technically a pet. But she was trained to be a therapy dog. She washed out of that, but she's still very intuitive. She knows when I need comfort. Or when I need her to chase trespassers." The last few words were spoken just as the grinder stopped, as if to emphasize her tease.

"Oh, ha ha." Matt rolled his eyes at her. "I still say she hates me."

"She didn't growl this morning."

He slid a spatula along the edge of the pan to

check the frittata. "She needed to pee. She was half-asleep."

"She was wide-awake the instant you broke that glass." Jillie pulled two plates down from the cupboard. "She's very in tune to my feelings. When I didn't trust you, *she* didn't trust you."

"So now you…trust me?"

She thought about it for a moment.

"I guess I do."

"I'm glad." He turned off the burner and stepped close, stopping right before his lips touched hers. "Is this okay?"

She nodded shyly and they kissed, only stopping when Sophie barked to come back inside.

He grimaced, turning back to the stove. "Like I said, your dog hates me."

They talked comfortably over breakfast. About Bryce's career. The crash on the Italian slopes in March that came perilously close to ending that career for good. The surgery to pin his femur back together. The need to take this winter away from competitive skiing so he could finish recuperating. That was why Matt bought an unknown ski lodge. To keep Bryce away from the party atmosphere of the popular ski towns.

She told him a little about her book—as much as she told anyone, which wasn't much. It was bad luck to talk too much about a work in progress. But they talked about the Shadow series, and, after they cleared the table—and kissed again—she did something she rarely did, even with friends. She showed him her office. He seemed to approve, running his hands along the built-in bookcases and admiring her view of the forest outside the window. The snow had stopped, but there was at least a six-inch coating of heavy wet stuff out there.

"This is pretty sweet," he said. "I'm glad you're far enough back that you can't see the lodge from down here." He slid his arm around her. "I wouldn't want to be responsible for disturbing the work of the great J.L. Cole." He kissed the top of her head. She could get used to this just-kissing thing.

"You didn't tell your brother about me."

"I promised I wouldn't. I keep my promises, Jillie."

She relaxed against him. His chest was solid on her cheek. She didn't *need* a protector, but still…it felt good to have a man like this at her side. Calm. Reliable. He hadn't rejected her when she couldn't give him what he'd clearly been ready for last night. But how long would he be satisfied taking things as slow as she needed?

Jillie's phone chirped on the counter. It was an alert from the security cameras—Chuck Jenner was headed up the long driveway, clearing the snow away with the big yellow plow on the front of his truck. She'd shown the photo to Matt when a text came in. It was from Bryce. The car was out of the ditch and at some body shop outside town. Bryce would be at Jillie's soon to pick up Matt.

He looked at Jillie, brows risen in question. "I can meet him at the lodge if you'd rather he not come up."

"It's fine. I doubt those shoes of yours are dry yet, and they already proved to be unreliable on snow. You'd probably fall down twenty times trying to get to the lodge."

He snorted. "You'd love that, wouldn't you?" He tapped a response on his phone. "I'll have him wait for me in the car. Looks like our little interlude is ending." They could hear the roar of the snowplow out front. His brows lowered, and he took her hand, winding his fingers through hers, like he did last night. "Jillie...I've enjoyed this. Spending time with you. I'd like to do it again." He grinned. "Maybe not wrecking my car, but us. Together."

"I'd like that, too. But I can't promise that I'll ever be ready...or when..."

He cupped the side of her face with his hand. "Stop worrying about what *isn't* happening. Let's just...take our time. And see what *does* happen. Okay?"

"Okay. How about dinner tomorrow night?"

He grinned, looking both surprised and pleased. "Sounds good. I'll do the cooking this time."

"You cooked breakfast!"

"My talents extend beyond the morning. I make a mean slow cooker brisket."

His phone chirped again. He looked so disappointed. "Bryce is here. We gotta see if those snow machines are going to do their job." He kissed her softly. "Thanks for everything. I'll see you tomorrow."

She watched him jog down the steps to Bryce's Jeep, her fingers on her lips. The lips that were already missing him.

"So you're telling me you and Jillie have basically been living somewhere between first and second base for two weeks now?" Bryce was rolling avocado paint on the wall behind the fireplace at the lodge. The wall that now separated the aprés-ski lounge from the newly outfitted kitchen.

Before Matt could answer, Asher Peyton spoke up from on top of a stepladder. He and Nate Thomas were hanging the last of the '60s-style satellite *chandeliers* Nate had found for the lodge. Nate's antiques and collectibles business was getting so busy it was starting to overtake his hardware business.

"Wow," Asher chuckled. "Sounds like someone's taking the long way *home*, if you catch my drift."

Nate nodded in agreement as he handed Asher the cordless drill. "First base is fun and all, but to *stay* there for two or three weeks? With a cutie like Jillie? I admire your restraint, man."

It was typical man-talk, razzing each other as pals did. Which was interesting, considering Matt and Bryce hadn't been here that long. He was learning that Gallant Lake was the type of town where, once you were trusted by one, you were trusted by all. And being trusted by Jillie Coleman was the gold standard. Her girlfriends and their men had quickly embraced Matt as one of their own. And they'd all embraced the idea of getting the ski slope open as soon as possible, jumping in to help. Christmas was coming fast, and it was beginning to look possible— after him declaring originally that it would never happen—that they might have a soft opening in time for some holiday break business.

He'd always intended to keep the midcentury-modern look of the place, with the funky orange-metal fireplace hood over the big flagstone hearth. It was interior designer Amanda Randall who'd suggested he go all in to embrace the look of the 1960s. As it all came together, he had to agree. The walls were variations of harvest gold and avocado, with one long wall of windows facing Jillie's place wall-papered in a retro wallpaper that brought it all to-gether. Amanda had found some deep-pile shag rugs to scatter around the lounge area, and it looked like Frank Sinatra might walk around the corner any minute with a martini in hand and some glamorous starlet on his arm.

"Uh-oh," Bryce laughed. "He's gettin' all uptight because we're talking about his girl."

He waved off the suggestion. "I'm ignoring you all. I've got other things to think about, like what else needs to be done to this place to get it open. But feel free to gossip among yourselves about something that's none of your business."

"Yup." Asher nodded, leaning into the screwdriver to secure the light fixture. "Uptight."

"Guys, I like Jillie."

"You like *kissing* Jillie…" Nate said.

"Yes, I do like kissing her." He liked that a lot. "I also like cooking dinner with her, and talking to her, and walking the dog with her and watching movies together…" They'd spent nearly every evening together since the storm, talking and snuggling and yes, kissing. Lots of kissing. He'd promised not to push her.

"And you're okay with that?" Asher came down off the ladder. "With going steady? I mean…I like Jillie and she's cute as hell. But won't you want more than that before much longer?"

"I already want more than that," Matt confessed. "But you know what she's dealing with. We're taking this at her speed."

"Has she been to the lodge yet?" Nate looked around the room. "This place is really looking great."

"I couldn't have done it without your help, guys.

And no, Jillie hasn't seen it. To be honest, I haven't asked her. I'm not sure she's ready." She'd tried to explain the *cascade* effect of her phobia, how a little stress could set off a fuse that suddenly led to full-blown panic. He wanted to respect it, even if he couldn't quite understand it. "Speaking of ready, is anyone ready for a shot of whiskey?"

The shiny new bar stretched along the far wall, parallel with the slopes outside. The thick glass shelves held bottles lined up right in front of the wide windows, which had been tinted, but you could still see straight out to the mountain. It made the area bright and open. All the fixtures were shiny chrome, in another nod to the midcentury look. He pulled out a bottle of top-shelf scotch and lined up four glasses.

Asher was the first to take a seat and accept a glass with a nod of thanks. "Nora said you're going to have quite the martini menu. That'll be something new for Gallant Lake."

"Well, you already have a beer joint in the Chalet, although we'll have some good craft beers on tap. We're going to do a whole '60s cocktail bar vibe, with updated twists on drinks like old fashioneds, whiskey sours and, of course, a fine selection of scotch."

Asher sipped his drink and smiled, lifting it in a toast. "I approve."

Bryce left, headed for the Chalet, where the

younger crowd hung out. Asher and Nate stayed and talked booze and restaurant menus. He'd hired an assistant manager out of Vermont, and Matt and Gary Connors were putting together a menu of simple pub fare, but with high-end ingredients. Black Angus burgers. Free-range organic chicken. Locally sourced produce whenever possible, of course.

Nate said he used to ski at the old lodge with Dan Adams back when they were teens, and the place had never looked this good back then. He hinted that he'd pulled out his old skis, but Matt shook his head. They needed another four or five days of cool weather and snowmaking. They hadn't had much natural snow since the storm, but it was cold enough, especially at night, to make snow nearly nonstop. The slopes were mostly white, but barely.

He and Bryce had already made a few passes down the mountain, testing out the base and the texture. Both were passable for now, considering they hadn't done any grooming and the base was thin to nonexistent in some places. He'd known going in that running a ski resort this far south in New York was a risky business.

Asher slid his empty glass across the bar, shaking his head at Matt's offer to refill it. "I gotta get back to my own mountain and get some sleep." He and Nora had a custom log home on the side of Gallant Mountain, straight across the lake, but not so straight to drive. Asher moved to stand. "I saw Bryce talking to Shane Brannigan the other day at the coffee shop. Looked pretty serious. Is Bryce thinking of hiring him?"

Matt tensed. "Hire him for what?"

He knew *what*, of course. Shane Brannigan was a well-known sports agent and client manager, with star athletes in multiple sports. Bryce had mentioned meeting him, but never mentioned sitting down with the guy. Nate and Asher looked at each other, picking up on the edge in his voice. He shook his head with a short laugh.

"Nothing like showing all my cards, huh? I know who Shane is and what he does. Bryce can make his own decisions, but right now *I'm* Bryce's manager."

"Sorry, man." Asher pulled on his jacket. "Didn't mean to spill the beans. For what it's worth, Shane's a great guy."

Nate nodded. "The best."

Matt took a breath and held on to it for a moment. The idea of Bryce actually following through and hiring someone else shook him more than he thought it would.

"I'm sure he's awesome. I just don't know if this is the right move for Bryce to make." He gave a harsh laugh and downed the rest of his drink. "Leave it to me to move my brother to the only small town in the world with a famous damn sports agent living in it. I'm really making stellar choices these days."

Nate clapped him on the back as they all headed to the door.

"They weren't all bad. You bought the only place next door to Jillie Coleman."

He laughed with them, but he couldn't help wondering if that was a good thing or not. How much longer could he be this close to her and stick to hand-holding and kisses?

Chapter Nine

Tiesha had been with Monica since the very beginning. They'd been children together in the idyllic fields of Rannabar, before the Shadows rolled down Stoneroot Mountain. Before the terror. Monica could ignore Robbie's advice. He didn't know her. But when Tiesha said it was time to snap out of it and fight, there was no way she could ignore that.

"One of these years I won't put so many decorations up for Christmas, but this is not that year." Amanda laughed as she set another box in the large hall at Halcyon, next to a towering tree.

Jillie looked up at the still-bare pine. "It's going to take us until Christmas to get the decorations up."

Nora peeked around the far side of the tree, a garland of tinsel draped around her shoulder. "This is the one time when my cousin out-plans even me. She'll have it done in a week. With a little help, of course."

Amanda put her arm around Jillie's shoulder and squeezed. "I'm so glad *you're* helping us this year."

Mel Brannigan, one of Amanda's other cousins, carried another box over and set it on a stack. "I'm glad, too! Someone else for Amanda to boss around. How did she trap you into it?"

Jillie laughed. "I think it was that extra serving of Thanksgiving turkey that lulled me into compliance."

It had been her second time joining the Randalls for Thanksgiving. She'd always been comfortable at Halcyon, and she knew everyone there—Blake and Amanda with their two children, Zach and Maddy. Mel with her husband, Shane, and their infant son, Patrick. Nora and Asher had been there last year, but this year they'd gone to North Carolina instead, to celebrate with another cousin and her family.

She helped the women drape pine garlands all around the house, on mantels and windowsills, tables and banisters. They set up a lovely nativity in the living room, with its windows overlooking the lake. They unboxed the tree ornaments, but set them out on tables, not on the tree. That was a task for another day, after Amanda supervised the lights being strung by workers from the resort, where holiday decorations were also going up this weekend.

While they decorated, they talked about holiday plans and what was happening in town—new businesses, new couples, kids getting into mischief, what the winter might be like. Jillie did far more listening than talking, and she knew they were fine with that. It felt good to have this little glimpse of…normal.

She didn't like that word, but it was hard to find any other way to describe a life that other people enjoyed without thought. A life she used to know. A life she'd told herself she didn't miss. She'd learned to cope with her agoraphobia by compromising with it, instead of fighting it. And that was fine. Except…

Jillie watched Amanda sweep her daughter Madeleine into her arms, laughing at the little girl who looked like Amanda's miniature. Nora and Mel were tossing tinsel back and forth at each other. Mack Adams arrived, apologizing for being late, and explaining she'd been busy with her stepdaughter Chloe. They were her friends, and this was Halcyon, but still…this was a noisy, chaotic scene that, even a year ago, would have had her tense and ready to bolt. But not today.

Mack held up a bottle of expensive wine. "I bring good tidings! My holiday inventory has arrived, including this beauty. Let's give it a taste, shall we?"

Amanda brought out some glasses and they gathered on the sofa and chairs near the marble fireplace.

Nora accepted a glass from Mack. "How was your Thanksgiving? I heard the Danzer brothers were with you?"

Jillie's head turned sharply. "They were?"

Mack nodded. "Dan felt bad that they didn't have anywhere to go, and Chloe was with her mom and stepdad for the day, so we had Matt and Bryce join us, along with our illustrious mayor Mary and her wife, Julia, plus Darius and the twins. It was definitely a friendsgiving meal."

"They are really nice guys," Mel said. "If anyone was going to open that ski lodge, I'm glad it was someone like Matt and Bryce. And my husband may end up with a new client out of the deal."

"Oh, Dan said something about Bryce and Shane talking. Is it serious?" Mack asked, nudging Jillie's shoulder. "If that happens, maybe Matt will stay in Gallant Lake. Wouldn't that be nice, Jillie?"

Her face heated. "It wouldn't affect me one way or the other."

That drew raised eyebrows and soft laughter.

"Sure." Amanda grinned. "Whatever you say. It's not like you haven't been making out with Matt Danzer for two weeks now."

"Whoa!" Nora held up her hand. "Define *making out*. Are you guys doing it?"

"No," Jillie answered. "I guess we *have* been taking it slow."

"I don't consider a few weeks as *slow*." Mack sipped her wine. "It's not a race. As long as you're both satisfied, who cares?"

That was the problem—she wasn't sure if they *were* both satisfied. Was Matt okay with their evenings at her place, spent watching movies or listening to music by the fire, highlighted with kissing? Lots and lots of kissing. Hell, she didn't know if *she* was satisfied. She just had no idea how to move forward. Would it spoil things? Would she panic? Would he be disappointed? She sat back with a sigh.

"How do I know if we're ready to explore going further?" She looked around at her friends. "How do I know if the timing is right?"

The women looked at each other with knowing smiles. Mack answered first.

"The fact that you're asking tells me it's time to go exploring."

"She's got a point," Mel agreed. "If you're thinking about it, what's stopping you?"

"You're okay with the kissing part?" Amanda asked. Jillie nodded. "Then take it a step at a time. Some heavy petting…" She giggled. "Do they still call it petting? You know, get a little physical, but with your clothes on…"

"We've done that." Jillie blushed again. "A few times."

The past few days had felt like they'd moved to a different level. More heat. More tension as they walked that fine line between taking it slow and throwing caution to the wind. More hands exploring, over and under clothing.

"Okay, then." Nora grinned. "Sounds like you're ready. As far as *how* to get there, just lead the man upstairs to your bed. I'm pretty sure he'll get the idea."

"You're saying *I* should initiate?" Jillie shook her head. "I am *way* out of practice."

"You've told him about your anxiety disorder, right?" Amanda squeezed her hand when Jillie nodded. "He may be waiting for *you*, then. Blake was super nervous the first time we…" She looked over to where her daughter was drawing a Christmas tree on a sketch pad and dropped her voice. "Well, you know. He'd seen my night terrors, and it spooked the hell out of him. You need to figure out a way to let him know you're ready."

"I agree," Mack said. "Matt may be content with the way things are, so don't do anything you don't want to."

"The thing is, I think he's as anxious to move forward as I am. We're in the friend zone and it… works, but that's not where we want to stay. Not where I want to stay."

Last night they'd stood at the door before he left, wrapped up in each other's arms, kissing each other senseless. He didn't want to leave. She didn't want him to go. But she didn't know how to ask him to stay.

"I hate to drink and run—" Mack stood with a sigh "—but I have another delivery coming in this afternoon. I agree with Nora—get that man near a bed and go for it." Her expression went soft. "He's one of the good guys, Jillie. I like him a lot. We all do."

"I know. I like him, too. A lot."

All she had to do was let *him* know that.

Matt finished drying the dishes and tucked the towel over the oven handle. That was the deal— whoever didn't cook cleaned up afterward. And tonight Jillie had made a chicken piccata that Matt thought put the world's finest chefs to shame. Of course, he might be a little biased.

They'd cleared the table together, continuing the dinner debate over the merits of *Star Wars* vs *Star Trek*. Matt was a diehard Trekkie like his dad had been. But Jillie, naturally for an author, liked the epic saga of *Star Wars*. Even if she didn't agree with the direction some of the films had taken, particularly with the female characters.

"Where do you want me to put this casserole dish?" He called the question out to her, not sure where she'd vanished to. Their routine was comfortable by now. Dinner, chitchat, argue about what movie to watch, sit by the fire or by the TV and cuddle together. Yup—he was officially a cuddler.

Never saw that coming.

Sometimes that was it…snuggling and a good-night kiss. Sometimes they started their kissing on the sofa and ended up laughing when neither of them paid attention to how the show ended. Sometimes it was just the two of them watching the fire, sitting on the floor together while they listened to music. Matt was a blues guy, but Jillie was pop all the way. They'd talk or, especially lately, kiss until he had to pull himself away and go home.

It was good. It was fine. He could be patient. He was a grown-ass man, for heaven's sake. And he had no desire to be the cause of a panic attack for her. So…first base was good. Fine.

Matt tossed a bag of popcorn into the microwave, since they'd decided this was a night for old school Hollywood horror—*The Hand.* Where a concert pianist's injured hand was replaced with the hand of a psychopath, and the hand was determined to keep killing. It was kitschy horror, but Jillie told him watching Saturday-afternoon horror flicks like that kept her distracted from the disaster her life often was as a kid. For her, the darkness of the old black-and-white movies was a safe place emotionally. It was her escape.

She joined him in the kitchen, Sophie at her heels. That explained where she'd been. The dog must have needed a nature call. When he turned around, juggling the hot bag of popcorn in his hands, she handed him a bowl, then turned away, suddenly pensive.

"Hey…" He poured out the steaming popcorn, then reached for her hand. "You okay? Would you rather watch a space flick tonight? You know, to prove your point about story arcs in outer space?"

Her mouth lifted a fraction on one side. Her cheeks flushed. "Actually, I thought we'd…um… try something different tonight." She took his hand, shaking her head when he reached for the popcorn bowl. "Why don't you leave that and come with me?"

He had no clue where she was taking him until they reached the bottom of the open staircase leading up to the loft. Up to her bedroom. He pulled back when she started up the steps. Was she for real right now? Was this just a "come look at my cool room" moment? He wasn't sure he could stand within sight of her actual *bed* without doing…something.

She turned when he stopped, standing one step above him, like she had that first night they'd kissed. That hint of a smile deepened into the real thing, her eyes darkening. She was sending a message he couldn't quite believe.

"Don't you want to come up?"

Matt couldn't stop his huff of disbelieving laughter. "Oh, I *want*, all right. But, babe…"

"Don't." She placed her fingers on his mouth. He couldn't help scooping them playfully in his lips as if to bite them, making her giggle. The smile grew more tremulous. "Come upstairs, Matt." She turned and started walking up ahead of him, her hips swaying seductively. She glanced back down at him from halfway up the stairs. "Unless you don't want to."

Matt was torn. He had no idea if this was a smart move or a disastrous one. There was no way he wasn't following her. The upstairs space was smaller, because it was tucked in the narrowing peak of the A-frame. It was still a spacious room, easily accommodating the king-size bed angled into one corner. From the bed, Jillie had a clear view out the sliding glass doors to a small balcony. She could also look down the mountain to Gallant Lake through the front windows.

The furnishings were sparse, with plenty of space to move around. A large oval braided rag rug, in a dozen pastel shades, anchored the setting. Jillie looked around, as if trying to see it through his eyes. Then she picked up a remote that was sitting on the dresser. She pressed a button and the blinds on the huge front windows closed.

"Show-off."

He liked to tease about her high-tech home, but his heart rate jumped at the thought of being closed in this room with Jillie. And that bed. He was still at the top of the stairs, not trusting himself to make

a move until he knew *for sure* what Jillie was expecting.

She walked to the bed and turned, looking surprised to see him frozen in place. She'd just led him
up to her bedroom. With a bed. A bed…right *there*.

"Matt? Are you okay?"

His mouth opened, but he stopped before saying
anything. She walked over to him.

"Do you want this?" She took his hand. Christ,
he wanted this with every fiber of his being.

"Pretty much more than anything in the world."

"So…?"

He owed her the truth. "I'm careening between
get her on the bed, you idiot and *slow down, you
idiot*." He tugged her closer, sliding his arm around
her waist. "As much as I want you, Jillie, I'm terrified of making the wrong move and…"

"And witnessing a panic attack."

Bingo.

"Well…yeah."

"I'm the one who led you up here. This—" she
gestured toward the bed "—is *my* idea. If anything
bad happens, it's on me, not you."

Matt nodded, stroking her hair with his hand.
"That sounds reasonable, babe, but I'm the one
who'll have to deal with it." He huffed out a laugh.
"I'm thirty-four years old, with a gorgeous woman
inviting me into her bed, and I'm *nervous*. Like…
schoolboy virgin nervous."

Jillie sobered. "That's my fault. I've spooked you with all my stories about my phobias and panic attacks."

She stepped away from him, moving closer to the bed. Her fingers traced the hem of her sweater, and she smiled. *Don't do it. Don't do it.* She grabbed the hem and tugged the sweater over her head, tossing it in the corner. Now she faced him in only her jeans and a pretty pink bra.

"Aw, hell, Jillie..." Matt groaned. "You're killing me here."

He wasn't kidding. His chest ached and his lungs burned from the effort it was taking not to go to her. She took a step closer to the bed, patting the mattress with her hand as if to test its acceptability. *Killing him.*

"What's it going to take, Matt?"

He finally moved out of his corner, walking over to where she stood by the bed. He cupped her face with his hands.

"What it's going to take is a promise that if we do this, and you start to feel a panic attack coming, you *tell* me. Right away. I don't know what to look for, so I may not notice. I need to be able to trust you to do that."

"Okay," she whispered, staring up into his deepening blue eyes. "Anything else?"

He blurted out all of his fears. "Tell me what I

should do if something does go wrong. I don't want to be left helpless. I need to know what to expect."

How could he make love to her if he had to watch her every move for a sign of a panic attack? That would be a mood killer, and he didn't want anything interfering with this moment.

Chapter Ten

"I stand before you tonight to tell you that it is time!" Monica slapped her sword against her shield, then held it high. The resistance army did the same, sending thunder echoing across the mountains.

How could Jillie reassure him without spoiling the moment any more than she already had? She'd considered leading him up here all week—even had the bed ready each night, but it wasn't until tonight that she'd found the courage to do it. What she hadn't anticipated was that his courage would be the prob-

lem. Matt was a caregiver, and it was tripping him
up to face a situation he might not be able to fix.

"If the worst happens and I panic…" She put her
hand over his against her cheek. "And I don't think it
will. I wouldn't have brought you up here if I wasn't
ready. But if it *does* happen…" She patted his hand,
knowing he was going to hate her answer. "There's
not much you can do, other than stay calm yourself
and let me work through it. Maybe call Sophie up.
She knows to cuddle into my lap and distract me.
She makes eye contact, and it helps keep me in the
present. Worst-case scenario, I end up rocking in the
corner trying to breathe." He started to pull back, but
she gripped his hand and stopped him. "That's the
worst case, Matt. You wanted honesty, and I'm giving it. It's not fatal. Even if I pass out, I won't die."

They stood in silence, the bed beckoning next
to them. She'd made the move to get them up here.
She'd answered his questions. It was up to him
now. His hands dropped to her hips, drawing her
up against him. She didn't react, waiting for the tur-
moil in his eyes to clear. This internal battle was his
to fight. Another moment passed, then his mouth
curved into the softest of smiles.

"I want you." He kissed her. "I want you in that
bed and naked against me. As long as you promise
not to die." He kissed her again, with more inten-
sity. His arms went around her, his fingers moving
against her skin, setting it on fire. His kisses traced

a path to her ear, his next words barely a breath. "If you're brave enough to stand here and take all this time reassuring me, then I'm sure as hell brave enough to do this…"

His hands slid up her back, still holding her tight against him. He deftly unhooked her bra, then slid the straps off her shoulders. He leaned back and watched as the bra fell from her breasts. A sharp breath—almost a hiss—escaped his lips. His hands moved to cup her breasts, and now it was her turn to hiss. It felt so good.

Her head fell back, eyes closed. She concentrated on the feel of his thumbs brushing her peaks gently, then pinching. It sent a sharp jolt of electrical current straight to her lower abdomen. He held her completely. Her breasts. Her heart. Her soul. His head dropped and he took her breast into his mouth, groaning as he tugged and nipped at her. Her knees trembled, but he caught her with one arm around her back, lowering her slowly to the bed without lifting his mouth from her.

He knelt on the mattress, holding her steady, pulling her farther onto the bed. She felt secure in his arms. And confident enough to do her own exploring. Her fingers went under his shirt, splaying against his skin and flexing against the hard muscles of his chest.

"Not fair," she murmured. "You still have too many clothes on."

"That's easy enough to fix." He straightened, tearing his shirt off with one hard motion. It landed on the floor near her sweater. He stared down at her with ice and fire in his eyes.

"You're so damn beautiful." His voice was thick with emotion. With desire. For her. It was a heady feeling to know that he wanted her. She grinned, sliding her hands up his chest and watching him shudder at his touch.

"You're not so bad yourself."

He reached down and cupped her breasts again, gripping them, kneading them, pinching them until she started writhing under him. He stared into her eyes, his smile deepening as she moved. He was straddling her, and she arched her back, desperate for more contact. He raised an eyebrow at her, still holding himself up, knowing full well he was stoking her need with his magic fingers.

Fine. She had fingers, too. They found his belt buckle and went to work, freeing first the belt and then his jeans. She slid them down over his hips. Her fingers pried under the waistband of his black boxer briefs, and soon they were down around his hard thighs, too.

And speaking of hard…she gripped him. His entire body jerked at her touch. His eyes were closed, and he was lost in sensation. No problem, because she was lost, too. Lost in the feel of him. In the power she had over him. In the desire rising up like a phoenix inside her—a fire she'd thought was gone forever.

"Wait…" Matt mumbled, sliding off the bed to finish shedding the rest of his clothing. He also grabbed a couple of foil packets from his pocket, one brow arching high when he saw her eyeing them. "Don't condemn me for having hope, babe."

She stretched on the bed, then lifted her hips so she could shimmy out of her jeans, nodding toward the nightstand.

"I wonder what they thought at the grocery store when *I* added condoms to my weekly shopping list for the first time in four years."

He laughed out loud at that. "So you were prepared, too?" She nodded with a playful grin, and he was still chuckling. "Hope springs eternal, eh?" He crawled back onto the bed, straddling her, grabbing a packet, and ripping it open. His smile fell slightly. "You okay with this?"

"I'm very okay with it."

And she was. She didn't want to examine that too much, for fear of ruining the moment. She reached up for him, and he obliged, lowering himself into her embrace. They lay like that, holding each other, feeling skin against skin, hearts racing in perfect rhythm.

He kissed her, hard and urgent, and his hips moved against her. She felt him settle between her legs and press. He stopped, as if waiting for permission. She granted it by rising up to meet him, and then…he filled her with one smooth motion. They froze, her fingers digging into his shoulder blades.

She wasn't sure who started to move first. It just happened. The only sound was their breathing, heavy and hard, quickening as their bodies quickened. She said his name. He said hers. Again. And again…louder now. The pace was intensifying. He grunted in her ear, groaning in what sounded like agony, but she totally understood. Because she felt it, too.

Something was building. Passion. Raw physical demand. She wanted the thrill of release as much as he did, but neither of them wanted this to end. It was a perfect agony. Fall, or try to hang on as long as they could. Her fingernails dug in harder. Behind her tightly closed eyelids, colors exploded like fireworks. Just a little bit longer…

"Jillie…I can't…are you…?"

She ran her lips down his neck, salty with sweat. "I'm ready…"

They exploded together. Jillie got lost in her head for a second, doing that writer thing where she puzzled about word choices. *Explosion* may be too mild a word for what just happened. Yes, a white-hot light seemed to fill the room for an instant. They'd both cried out. They'd both spiraled back to earth clasping each other. Kissing whatever skin was available— neck, shoulder, ear, jawline. Her insides felt like jelly, and her whole body trembled like a freshly struck bell. No simple explosion could do all that, right? Maybe the force of neutrons colliding in a controlled environment…no, there was nothing controlled about where they'd just gone in her bed. *Explosion* was inadequate. But she had no other word that came close. She shuddered, and Matt let out a long, low groan.

"Holy… What the… Baby, I…" Clearly, he was having the same problem with words that she was. His head dropped to her shoulder, his weight covering her like a warm, weighted blanket. Her own personal ThunderShirt. His lips moved against the skin at the base of her neck. "All I can say is…wow."

She ran her fingers through his hair, sweeping it off his forehead and looking deep into his eyes. "Excellent word choice."

He huffed a laugh against her. "I know I'm crushing you, but…give me a minute, okay? I seriously don't think I can move right now. I think you turned me into one of your stone monsters, rooted straight into the mountain."

"Hmm," she murmured, still stroking his hair. "Maybe this is how my heroine Monica should defeat them…just sex them into submission."

"That would definitely be a book I'd read, but the rest of your fans might be a bit shocked."

She was tracing her fingers up and down his back now. They were both covered with a thin sheen of sweat. From exertion. From adrenaline. He kissed her shoulder and started to move to one side.

"I'd be happier if we kept this magic trick to ourselves, though. Just because I'm falling for a writer doesn't mean I want to show up in your books." He'd managed—with one more groan—to slide off her. But one arm and one leg still draped across her, weighing her down. Maybe he knew she needed to be held down or she'd float away like a dandelion ball of feathery seeds.

He propped his head on one arm, looking down into her face. "You haven't answered me."

She frowned, trying to remember what question he'd asked. Then she realized it wasn't exactly a question, but a statement he'd wanted her to reassure him about. Her smile returned.

"It's an occupational hazard of dating a writer, Matt. We are always looking for fresh material and plot bunnies." He hadn't used the word *dating,* though. He'd said he was *falling for* a writer. Falling for her. Her heart did a quiet little somersault in her chest. She stuck with the safer subject of writing. "I was given a T-shirt once that said 'I'm a writer— anything you do or say could end up in my book.'"

He nodded, unfazed. "Fair enough. Will you at least be generous in your descriptions of me? You know…best sex you ever had in your entire life and all that…" Matt's face fell, and Jillie knew her past had just reentered the relationship. She raised her head to kiss him, long, soft and sweet.

"Don't do that. Don't pre-edit your words around me. If I don't like something you say, I'll tell you. I won't hold it against you. I'm not looking for ways to bring my trauma front and center all the time. I'm *not*." She stared straight into his eyes, wanting him to feel the truth of what she was saying, even as she tried to lighten the moment. "I've paid therapists a whole lot of money to make sure that one tragedy doesn't define me."

He flopped onto his back, staring up at the ceiling and muttering to himself. "I'm blowing this, aren't I? All night I've been the one acting like an anxious victim, anticipating…whatever. I'm the one who keeps inviting this damn conversation about stuff you don't want to talk about…"

"Whoa. Easy there, big guy." She patted his shoulder. "This is new for you. But it's just another day in the life for me."

He opened one eye and slid his gaze her way. "Well, so much for my ego." He put his hand over his heart in a show of despair. "*Just another day.* And here I thought we had some stellar, lifetime-goals sort of sex tonight. But sure…just another day…"

Giggling, she scrambled to lie on top of him, staring down at his face as he held her there.

"I was most definitely *not* referring to the sex, and you know it. The sex was…" She paused, then shook her head. "As a writer, I am rarely unable to describe something, but what we did defies description, Matt. It was even better than I'd dreamed, and I dreamed about it, believe me." She tapped his nose playfully. "How's that for your manly ego? I dreamed about making love with you."

He chuckled. "That definitely helps the ego, thanks." His hand stroked her back, holding her above him. "And that sparkle in your eyes helps, too. You look like a satisfied woman."

She pretended to think for a moment, staring up into the air. "Hmm…yeah, I guess you could say I'm satisfied." She buried her face against his neck. Emotions were coming at her fast and furious, and she wasn't sure how to handle it. Even *good* stress was still…stress. And she wasn't sure how to deal with the fact that she already wanted to do it all over again. "And a tired one."

He hesitated. "Do you want me to go?"

"No." Her quick answer surprised them both. She thought about it, then repeated herself. "No, I don't want you to go, Matt."

"Good." He rolled over so she was under him again. He kissed her hard and long. "Are you too tired to…?"

As much as she *thought* she needed time to process, she answered the question before he finished asking.

"I'm not too tired for that. In fact, I was worried you might not ask."

"Cut me some slack, Jillie. Men don't bounce back quite as fast as women do. But you've worked some magic on me, because there's nothing I'd rather do right now than make love to you again."

Matt watched as the soft light of morning slid into the loft and across Jillie's sleeping face. Despite the peaceful silence, he knew his life had just been riotously upended. Making love to Jillie Coleman for one single night had changed…everything.

He reached out to sweep a strand of dark hair from over her eyes. She murmured something and wrinkled her nose before sighing back into a deep and contented sleep. How could she be anything *but* contented after the night they'd just had? That wasn't just his ego talking—although, the soft smile on those kiss-swollen lips made him feel damn proud. They'd laughed and loved for hours on end. Whispering sweet words, then crying out. Tracing fingers gently across sweaty skin, then holding tight to keep from falling into a whirl of sensation that seemed both dangerous and oh, so tempting. Exploring…constantly exploring. And wanting to do it all over again, just in case they'd missed some tantalizing spot.

A soft quilt covered her lower body, but his eyes were able to leisurely take in her breasts, her ivory skin, her cocoa-colored hair and lips of dusty rose.

She was the most beautiful thing he'd ever seen, without question. His forehead gathered. But what now?

Sure, he'd been fascinated by his bossy, uptight neighbor from the start. She was clever and fun to talk to, even when they were arguing. They liked the same books and movies and stuff, for the most part. They were…compatible. She was a *lot* of fun to kiss. His fingers brushed her lips, making her flinch and sigh again in her sleep. The sound shot through him like electricity. Damn, he wanted her *again*. Before now, he'd have said he wasn't physically capable of this many repeats in one night. Jillie was turning a lot of his assumptions upside down.

Like the one where he thought his life had a predetermined path. Raise Bryce. Protect Bryce. Manage Bryce's career. Move every few years in order to do that properly. No entanglements. He huffed a soft laugh at that one, looking down at Jillie. She had him tangled up so tight he could barely see that plan anymore. He couldn't see his future…at least not a future without her in it.

It's not like he ever made a conscious decision to be a lifelong bachelor back when he'd vowed to be his brother's parent, adviser, chaperone and bodyguard. That was just the way it happened. And he'd been doing it for so long now. Would Jillie join them on the ski tour? Highly unlikely, with her phobias. Could Bryce behave himself out there without Matt nearby? Unlikely, but…maybe. Nah. The kid had always had a wild streak. More than a stranger like Shane Brannigan could be expected to handle.

A soft touch to his cheek snapped him out of his musing with a start. Jillie's fingers traced along his bottom lip. She was smiling up at him.

"You look very serious for someone who…well, you know."

"For someone who just had the best night of his life?" The corner of his mouth lifted. "I was enjoying watching you sleep."

"Try again. You were a million miles away. What were you thinking about?"

He stared at her, then sighed. "Life. The world. Random big thoughts like that." He kissed her forehead. "That's what rockin' sex does, you know. Makes you examine your place in the universe."

She pressed her lips together, holding back a smile. "Wow. All it does for me is make me sleepy." She looked around the room, which was brightening as the sun began sliding up over the mountain on the far side of the lake. "And hungry."

His eyes slid across her bare chest again, and he pulled her closer, speaking against her lips.

"Yeah, I'm hungry, too."

Her laugh was husky and downright erotic in his ears.

"Again? Are you a superhuman who doesn't need sleep?"

"Who needs sleep when I can reenergize just by looking at you?"

Her eyes went soft, then closed as he kissed her hard and deep. Their bodies came together this time as if they'd been lovers for years. No surprises. Knowing what the other needed. Natural. Sexy as hell. And ultimately, both explosive and satisfying.

Two things dragged them out of bed an hour later. Hunger and Sophie. The dog had begrudgingly stayed on her bed downstairs as ordered, but her persistent whine told them she'd run out of patience and bladder strength.

Jillie cooked French toast for breakfast, sprinkling it with sugar before turning it, like they did in Europe. When he asked about it, she told him she'd spent a summer traveling around Europe with college friends. His eyebrow rose, and she shook her head at him as she refilled their coffee mugs, then sat back down.

"I told you I was a completely different person back then, Matt. My coping mechanism was to drown my issues in booze, parties and…random sex. The easy girl is the popular girl." She lifted her shoulder. "That's what I told myself, anyway."

"Until you saw him in Philly that night."

She went still. "Yes."

"Then you became a recluse. Instead of burying your past with noise, you buried it with silence."

She gave him a half smile. "That's a good way to

put it. They say every coping mechanism is valid in its own way. Our minds create ways to avoid pain." She straightened, then reached for his empty plate. "And why are we talking about this now? Surely, there are happier things on our minds after the night we had."

Matt joined her at the sink. "Okay. Let's talk about last night. I don't know about you, but I'd really like last night to happen again." She paused. He noticed her gripping the sponge tightly. Was she going to say one night was all she could handle? Would *more* be too much for her? She reached for his hand.

"I'd like that, too. I…I don't want to examine this too hard, though. Not yet. Can we keep this just…?"

"Random sex?" He knew the words, meant as a joke, were a mistake as soon as they left his lips. She physically recoiled, pressing her lips together in a thin line.

"God, Matt, is that what you think? That I do this sort of thing…"

He took the breakfast plate from her hand and set it in the strainer, then pulled her into an embrace. "Of course not. Sorry. That was a bonehead thing to say. I keep putting my foot in my mouth when I talk about your…"

"My affliction?" She smiled up at him, and it softened the sting a bit. "Like I told you last night, I get it. I'm used to living with my coping methods. You're not."

"Yeah, but I usually have a little more class than that. I'm so afraid of making it worse, but I'm blundering all over the place doing exactly what I'm trying to avoid." He hesitated. "It's hard to understand. I don't know what to expect, or when, or what might trigger it. We went wild last night and it felt like the most natural thing in the world. But if I invited you to *my* place…hell, I can't even get you to walk into the lodge."

Bright spots of pink rose on her cheeks. She didn't meet his gaze, and instead, stared over his shoulder at some imaginary target.

"I never said it would be easy being my friend. Or my lover." Now her eyes slammed into his. "This is me, Matt. You should do an internet search on agoraphobia before we go any further with…this. With us. Every case is different, of course, but you'll get a feel for the reality of it." Her lips pinched together for a moment. "As far as your house or the lodge goes, there are some agoraphobes who literally can't step out their own doors. You already know I'm able to go to some places, with certain people, under certain circumstances. I'm sure we can figure something out, with minimal people around, but I'm always going to need an escape route."

"But it's not like you're going to run into…him… at the ski lodge."

"You can't really promise that, can you?"

"Come on, what are the odds…?" He was arguing logic against a psychological condition that didn't operate on logic at all. "Okay. You're right. But can't doctors help you somehow? You said there were ways…"

"I've accepted this as part of who I am. It's what I do to keep myself feeling safe."

"But…I want to keep this going, Jillie. I want us to be a couple. A relationship. That means going out to dinner and traveling and…"

"Does it?" Her smile faltered. "If that's a require-ment, then I'm afraid we're not going very far."

His mouth opened a few times, then snapped shut. He tried to be an open-minded guy but dating some-one who never left home was going to be tough. Jillie's face fell, interpreting his silence as agree-ment. Being with *this* woman was worth him mak-ing adjustments to his thinking and behavior. After all, what was the big deal if she didn't come to his place? It was just a rental, and Bryce was there, so her house made more sense, anyway.

"Babe, I'd move into a bear's den up on Watcher Mountain if that's what it took to be with you. I'm going to be clumsy with my words once in a while, or anxious about doing the wrong thing, but I prom-ise…" He kissed her lips gently, tracing more kisses down her neck to the soft skin by her shoulder. "I promise I'll never *intentionally* hurt you. I want us to move forward…together. I'm falling for you, Jil-lie. And it started long before last night."

Tension left her shoulders and she pressed close against him, wrapping her arms around his waist. "I'm falling, too, Matt. I promise to cut you some slack if you stumble. And I'll stumble, too, you know. I have no real experience with this relationship stuff." They stood there for a moment, quiet and at peace in each other's arms. He wanted this to last forever. If only…

He grimaced. "I've got to go, babe. All the new glassware is supposed to be delivered today, and Bryce and I need to set up the bar. With any luck, and some cool weather, we might be able to have a soft opening between Christmas and New Year's. That and the winter break in February are the big money-making weeks for ski slopes in the northeast, where the seasons can be short." Matt chuckled. "Sorry, didn't mean to go into work mode on you in the middle of a conversation about us."

She stepped back with a smile. "Believe it or not, you're not the only one with a job to worry about. I have a deadline coming up, and my characters are misbehaving very badly right now. So let's both get to work." She raised a brow in question. "Will I see you tonight?"

"You know you will. I'll bring dinner. And a toothbrush."

They both laughed at that, making something go warm and soft in the vicinity of his heart. She patted his chest. Yup. Right there.

"And a toothbrush," she agreed.

Chapter Eleven

Her friends said she could trust the shadowy hulk waiting at the edge of the trees. Even Robbie insisted that this monster was different. That this one might be able to bring peace to their land once again. She rubbed her eyes in exhaustion. She could barely remember what peace felt like.

"He wants to go out on a date."

Mel chuckled. "Well, that *is* the natural progression of things…oh…I didn't think…it's the going *out* that's a problem." Her nose wrinkled. "Sorry. Is there a place that you could manage?"

"You could come here," Nora said, gesturing around the Gallant Brew.

Jillie stared into her coffee mug. "I think he has something a little more formal than a coffee shop in mind." She looked up. "No offense."

Nora laughed. "I was kidding." She sobered. "But what *are* you going to do?"

That was a really good question. Matt's request that morning had caught her off guard. She could have said no and let that be that. After all, he knew it was a big ask of her. Going out, into a public place, on a *date*. But there was something in his eyes—caution mixed with hope—that had made her nod mutely in reply. And he'd run with that agreement, not giving her a chance to think twice. Kissing the top of her head as he walked past her at the kitchen island, saying a quick goodbye and vanishing out the front door with a happy smile.

She sighed. "I think he wants a *real* date. Like dinner at the Chalet or something."

Amanda sat back, shaking her head. "We all know that's not happening. The Chalet on a Friday night will be pure chaos, especially right before Christmas. What if I reserve you that corner booth at Gallante? You know, the one that's kind of hidden behind the bar? It's right up against the windows so it feels open."

It wasn't a bad idea. Gallante was the upscale restaurant inside the Gallant Lake Resort. She'd met

Amanda there a few times for a late lunch, when the restaurant was quiet. The wall of windows facing the lake gave the feeling of being outdoors. But the restaurant would not be quiet in the evening. The resort was a popular tourist getaway, especially for those looking to get out of New York City for a pre-Christmas escape. And the locals also frequented Gallante, since it was the only show in town for fine dining.

Yes, it would be difficult for her. But Matt had been working so hard. And he wanted so much to be out in public with her. He hadn't pressured her outright about it, but he kept dropping suggestions that it "would be nice." She picked up her phone and texted him.

How about Gallante for tonight? Amanda can make reservations.

The answer was swift.

Perfect. Make it for seven and I'll pick you up.

She looked at Amanda with her bravest smile.

"Book that table for seven o'clock."

Amanda made a face as if whistling in surprise. "You got it. Do you want me to hang around the restaurant, just in case you need…anything?"

"Nope. I'll be fine."

None of her friends looked like they believed that, but she was going to give it her best shot.

Six hours later she and Matt stood in the parking lot of the Gallant Lake Resort. The entire fieldstone-and-timber hotel was twinkling with Christmas lights. Thick pine garlands draped over the massive front doors and down the sides of the stairs. It looked like a holiday card.

It was terrifying.

Matt leaned over and whispered, his breath hot across her ear. "We don't have to do this."

She pressed her lips tightly together. She'd come this far. The man wanted a date. She wanted the man.

"I'm okay. I mean…I'm *not* okay, obviously. I can't move. But we're here. All I have to do is get through the lobby. The restaurant will be better. Just let me gather my thoughts…"

Matt chuckled, sliding his arm through hers and drawing her to the side, away from the doors. "I meant we don't have to go through the front doors. Or through the lobby. Come on." He looked down at her feet. "I'm glad you wore sensible shoes."

"They're not *that* sensible." She'd changed into this pantsuit from the dress she'd tried on first. She hadn't worn a dress in years, and thought it might make her feel too anxious. She had enough anxiety as it was. So the trim black wool suit and blue silk blouse would have to do. Just because her ankle boots were…well…boots, that didn't mean they were *sensible*.

"That wasn't an insult, babe." Matt led her down the sidewalk in front of the hotel and then off into the frost-covered grass. "They're very pretty and I can't wait to slide them off your feet later tonight and kiss my way up your leg. But I think five-inch stilettos would have been challenging on the lawn."

"Where are we going? And what would you have done if all that snow hadn't melted this week?"

He gave her a playful scowl. "Don't mention the M-word. There will be no more melting talk until after the holidays. I need to be able to make snow next week." She rolled her eyes but nodded in agreement.

"Fine, but you still haven't said where we're going." She hurried to keep up with him on the slippery frozen grass. "We have reservations at Gallante. Amanda took care of it."

He grinned down at her. "You're not the only one with connections in this place. Blake left a side door open for us. It's normally for deliveries, but at night he said the hallway would be quiet."

They stopped by the nondescript door, braced open just a fraction with a small stone. It was a good thing, since there was no handle on the outside. She was giggling when they stepped inside.

"I feel like a spy! Or a thief." She watched as he kicked the stone away and let the door close securely.

"I promised Blake I wouldn't invite any actual thieves inside after we got here." He put his arm around her shoulder. "You okay?"

The hallway wasn't pretty. Cement floor and white walls, with long fluorescent lights on the ceiling. It sloped gradually upward. It was wide and, most important, empty. So much better than the lobby, which would have been crowded and noisy with holiday tourists. And probably more than she would have been able to handle. She smiled.

"I'm definitely okay. This is brilliant."

He swelled with pride, clearly pleased with himself.

They went down another, smaller hallway, then through a door that opened into a public area, but a quiet one. The floor was carpeted, and the walls shimmered with metallic gold wallpaper. There was a woman checking her coat at the coatroom, laughing with the young woman inside. Jillie clutched Matt's hand, and he squeezed in acknowledgment but didn't slow. Two more turns, a few more people, and they were inside the restaurant at last. The hostess acted as if she'd been watching for them, grabbing two menus and hurrying to lead them back into the far corner, near the windows and away from other diners. Jillie slid into the booth and let out a long breath, then started to laugh.

"What's so funny?" Matt was watching her carefully, probably wondering if laugher was a sign of impending doom.

"It's a writer thing. We tend to roll our eyes when book characters do cliched things like letting out a breath they didn't know they'd been holding. But that's exactly what I just did. I didn't know I was holding my breath while we walked through the restaurant, until I sat down and let it out with a *whoosh* like a leaky tire!"

"But you're okay?"

"Seriously, Matt, if you're going to ask me that every five minutes we may as well go home."

He promised to stop, but she knew he was still nervous. Hell, she was nervous. This was a hug step for her. They both relaxed as their meal went on. They forgot about the other people and stared out the window at the lights twinkling in the trees leading to the lakeshore. Their conversation grew less hesitant, and by the time their elegant desserts were served, they were arguing about whether his apple fritter topped with cinnamon ice cream was better than her chocolate rum cake with raspberry sauce.

"Come on, it's Christmas in the Northeast," Matt exclaimed. "What's more authentic than apple pie or an apple fritter?"

Jillie waved her fork at him. "Maybe for Thanksgiving, but Christmas is a time for over-the-top desserts. Look how pretty this is!" She gestured toward the towering cake.

"Hmm. Pretty is as pretty does." Before she could react, he reached out and snagged a large forkful of *her* cake.

"Hey!" She retaliated by stealing a bite of his apple fritter. They laughed and agreed that *both* desserts were pretty amazing. It wasn't until they were drinking their after-dinner cognac that Jillie felt her first twinge of panic. It was her own fault. She'd started to mentally pat herself on the back for doing so well. Which, of course, opened the door to thinking about all the reasons she was doing well, like Matt's company and the way he made her feel. It also opened the door to all the reasons she should *not* be doing so well. She was sitting in a crowded restaurant on a Friday night for the first time in years. There were strangers all around her, including a noisy cluster of younger couples at the bar. They'd had too much to drink. They were…unpredictable.

And *unpredictable* was never a good thing for her. *Unpredictable* was dangerous. What if they moved closer? What if they came to the table…*why* would they come to the table? It didn't matter. If they came any closer, they might block her access to the door. Even if they didn't, she'd never make it across the full restaurant to the main doors, where more laughing people were gathered. What if she couldn't get to the outside? What if she passed out right here, in front of Matt? Would he be disgusted? Would he be embarrassed? Would he stop seeing her?

"Jillie?" His voice sounded as if it was in an echo chamber. She blinked and looked at him, but it was like looking through binoculars the wrong way. A narrowing tunnel surrounded by darkness. He spoke again, and she knew the words, but she was having a hard time understanding. "All right," he said calmly. "Let's get out of here. Everything's okay. I've got you." She was aware of his arm around her waist. Her coat over her shoulders They were walking. He was speaking to other people, but everything was a blur to her. Colors. Lights. Shadows. A burst of laughter ahead of them, then they were past it. They were in an echoing hallway now…and then they were outside.

The shock of the cold air helped make her more alert. Still, her legs buckled. Matt swept her into his arms, carrying her around the hotel and back to his car. The whole time he was murmuring words of comfort in her ear. Promising she was okay. Promising to protect her. Telling her…wait…

Did he just say he *loved* her?

If the cold made her alert, *that* word snapped her right to attention.

Matt stopped by his car, Jillie in his arms. Her panic attack came out of nowhere, after a near-perfect dinner date. Just because he'd stopped *asking* if she was okay didn't mean he'd stopped watching her closely. The first signs had appeared after dessert. One minute she'd been laughing and stealing his apple fritter, and the next minute her eyes were going glassy as she started looking around the room.

That was when he knew there was a problem. She'd ignored the restaurant until that moment. Until then, it was as if it was just the two of them in an intimate little bubble. As soon as she became aware, her pupils began to dilate, her breathing became more rapid, her color paled. He'd already given his credit card to the server, so he went by instinct. He ushered Jillie away from the table, hurried her out the back door and got her outside where it was safe. Carrying her to the car without falling was no easy feat in the icy grass, but he'd managed. He could tell she was coming back to him. Calming down, snuggling into his arms.

And then he blurted out the words. He was trying to calm her, that was all. But the declaration slipped out.

I love you.

It was fruitless to hope she hadn't heard, because he'd felt her whole body go completely still. He let her legs slide down until she was standing there in front of him. There was no point in pretending.

He put his arms around her and nodded at her shocked expression.

"It's true. I've fallen in love with you, Jillie. Don't ask me how or why or when. I know it as much as I know I'm right-handed. I love you."

Her mouth fell open, and then she began to laugh. Loudly. Almost hysterically. Had he just triggered another panic attack? Then she rested her hand on his chest, her laughter growing lighter. More genuine. Which oddly didn't help, because she was still laughing *at* him.

"This isn't exactly the reaction I expected..." He frowned. "I just told you that..."

"Oh, I heard you. But Matt..." She wiped dampness from her cheek. "Your timing is just...too much. It's all a little fuzzy, but I'm pretty sure I just had a full-on panic attack in the middle of our date."

He shrugged. "Technically, it was the *end* of the date. And I'll have to take your word for it being full-on. You didn't pass out or anything. You got... uptight. So I got us out of there. No big deal."

"Oh, I'm pretty sure it was a big deal. I'm quite sure you've never had a date quite like that."

"That's true." He kissed her forehead. "For example, I've never told a woman I loved her and been laughed at." He tipped her chin up to stare straight into her eyes. "I've never told a woman I loved her. Period."

She smiled, her eyes sparkling brighter than the Christmas lights on the resort. "Okay, maybe it wasn't a full-on anxiety attack, but it was close. You didn't freak out, though. You just...took care of it. And yes, you said you loved me. And for some weird reason, I think I love you, too."

Matt heard the words. But his brain refused to accept them. He wanted it. He wanted her to love him. But what did that mean for them?

"You…you what?"

"We love each other, Matt." She chuckled. "So… now what?"

They stared at each other in stunned silence, in the middle of a parking lot. She reached up to cup his face with her hands. "We don't need to solve this tonight. Let's hang on to the wonderful parts of the evening and see what comes next. One day at a time, like we have been. We can do that, right?"

And they did do that. They got through Christmas, spending it with the Randalls at Halcyon. It was a big family holiday unlike any Matt had experienced as an adult. Bryce had played video games with Zach, and gave little Maddy a ride on his shoulders, galloping around the big old house.

They got through the holiday break, which flew by with him working nearly nonstop at the ski slope. The week was thankfully cold enough to make plenty of snow, and word had gotten out to Gallant Lake and the towns around them that the old ski resort was open for business. They'd done solid business right through New Year's.

He still made it to Jillie's nearly every night, but there were some evenings when he fell asleep as soon as he hit the mattress. She didn't seem to care.

She'd crawl in bed with him and hold him until morning. They hadn't spoken of love again. But he felt it. He was sure of it. More sure every day. It should be a happy thing. Love was supposed to be *happy. It solved everything, right?* That's how it worked in the movies.

But here in the real world, he didn't see how those solutions played out. Bryce's leg was feeling better. He was making noises about flying out to an event at Lake Louise in January. He said it was to catch up with friends, but the doctor had cleared him, and Matt knew Bryce was itching to compete. Which meant travel. Which meant Matt would be leaving Jillie behind. For weeks at a time.

He'd eventually put the ski lodge up for sale, as planned. Leave Gallant Lake, as planned.

None of those plans worked if he and Jillie were in love. How could he leave her? How could he let Bryce go back to competing without him? Which was more important—his love for Jillie or his responsibility to his brother? He'd sworn on his parents' graves, for God's sake.

He was still struggling with all those questions when he and Jillie joined their friends one mid-January weekend. They'd all gathered at the Brannigan house for a chili party. Everyone brought different toppings and sides—cornbread, noodles, cheese, tortilla chips.

But as Matt stood near the family room bar of

the rambling new lakeside home, staring between Bryce and Shane Brannigan, he was realizing two things. First, there was more to Bryce's presence at this gathering than just chili. And second, his plans, as scattered as they were, had just been obliterated.

Outside, a large yellow Lab was careening through the snow, bounding between Amanda Randall and Nora Peyton. Nora's grandson George was toddling around in his snowsuit, laughing every time the dog knocked him over with her swinging tail. Amanda and Blake's six-year-old daughter Maddy was trying to protect George, but that wasn't going all that well, because she kept laughing and falling down into the fluffy white stuff, too. Blake Randall and Nora's husband, Asher, were talking to each other at the end of the shoveled-off patio, each holding a beer and watching the kids with wide grins.

Jillie was out there, too. She stood on the patio with Shane's wife, Mel, laughing at the antics, then gesturing for Sophie to leave her side and go join the fun. Sophie and the other dog—Matt thought her name was Nessie—were clearly pals, and soon they were rolling around in the snow as the two children played together. A frozen Gallant Lake shimmered silver in the background. It was a quintessential American family scene. A genuine Christmas card moment. It was *family*. And Matt felt completely disconnected from it.

"This is a *good* thing, Matt." Bryce's voice

seemed to be coming through a tunnel. Matt shook his head to clear the cobwebs, then turned back to the two men. His brother and his brother's new manager. Bryce licked his bottom lip. He always did that before breaking through the gates on a new ski slope, especially if the conditions were challenging. These were the things Matt knew about Bryce. And Shane didn't.

Shane cleared his throat. "I can assure you I have Bryce's best interests in mind. We'll take care of him as if he was *our* brother."

"But he's *not* your brother, is he?" Matt wasn't sure why he was so angry, but rage…or panic…rose up inside him. "You've been wining and dining him and impressing him with your New York offices and fancy clients, as if a baseball player's career has anything in common with a downhill skier."

Bryce started to argue, but Shane stopped him with a shake of his head before answering Matt. "You're not the first family member I've replaced as manager. I get it. The emotions of the job and the emotions of the relationship get all tangled up together until you're not sure where one ends and the other starts." Shane rested his hand on Bryce's shoulder, and Matt had to look away. "Bryce will *always* be your brother. Nothing about that relationship changes. He needs your support. He needs you behind the lines, cheering him on. He needs to be able to talk to you about what he's thinking and

who's getting on his last nerve and why that pretty
forest ranger keeps showing up at the Chalet the
same time Bryce does."

Matt's brow rose at that, and Bryce's cheeks red-
dened. Had he missed a relationship blooming between Bryce and Holly? He frowned. Maybe he
hadn't been paying as much attention to Bryce and
his rehabilitation as he should have been. Which
made him both a bad manager *and* a bad brother.

"We need this," Bryce said. "You don't need to
be my parent anymore. You don't need to be my
manager anymore. Just be my big bro." He grinned
and winked at Matt. "And frankly, Shane's already
made me more money than you ever did."

"What are you talking about?" Matt had worked
a few sponsorship deals for Bryce through the years,
when companies approached them. Some had been
fairly lucrative, but most of those went away when
Bryce got kicked off the US team.

"I've got a few contacts in the fashion world,"
Shane explained. "The folks at Clarity Sports Apparel are very interested in having an edgy young
skier wearing their logo. And we've got a tequila
company ready to sign Bryce right now for some
commercials. I think he's a natural for TV with his
quick smile and big personality."

"Television?"

"And online. They've got some ideas for a series
of short videos telling an ongoing story on their web-

site. They were going to go with a tennis star, but that fell through, and it's a great fit for Bryce. I'm trying to get him into some announcer booths this winter as a commentator. The collegiate games up in Lake Louise may present some opportunities to test the waters."

Matt swallowed hard. Tequila? Television commercials? Apparel? There was no way he'd know how to land sponsors like that.

"Shane said we should film some ads at the ski lodge!" Shane straightened, but Bryce didn't seem to notice. "They need shots of me on the slopes, so why not shoot them here, right?"

Shane seemed uncomfortable with Bryce's enthusiastic outburst. *Get used to it, pal.* He cleared his throat. "It's a possibility, but first we need signed contracts. And that means…" He glanced at Matt.

"That means you need me out of the way."

Shane barked out a laugh. "Well, that's not exactly the way I'd put it. You're still part of his decision-making. Part of his life. A permanent unpaid adviser, if you will." He grew somber. "My partner Tim and I have been doing this for a long time now. Our agency is small. We only take on clients we feel will be a good fit for us. Once they're on board, we work our asses off for them." The corner of his mouth lifted. "And that fancy New York office you think I dazzled him with? It's a third floor office above my wife's boutique on Main Street. Tim runs our office in Brooklyn, near his husband's business, but it's hardly fancy." He leaned his hip against the mahogany bar, watching through the window as his wife, Mel, laughed at something Jillie said. "There was a time when I wanted the corner office on the fortieth floor, but I came to my senses. Tim and I aren't in it for the flash. We're in it for what we can do for our clients."

Matt stared at Bryce. "He's known as the bad boy of skiing, you know."

Shane grunted. "Bad boys and wild children have somehow become our specialty. We usually manage to keep them on the straight and narrow…or at least under the radar." The soft sounds of a baby beginning to stir came from the small white speaker sitting on the bar. Shane stood and tapped the window, waving at his wife. "My son awakens. Do you guys need to talk more about this? I don't need an answer tonight, you know, but…"

Matt turned to Bryce. "This isn't my decision. It's yours."

There was a brief moment of desperation in his brother's eyes. For one brief instant, he looked like the uncertain young boy he'd once been. And just as fast, the look was gone. The man was back. He gave a short nod at Matt, as if to accept the mantle of adulthood once and for all. He stood, extending his hand to Shane.

"Let's do this."

Chapter Twelve

Tiesha laughed at Monica. "You're falling for that boy."

"Don't be silly. Robbie's a good soldier. That's it. A comrade, and nothing more."

"Okay. You keep telling yourself that."

Jillie knew Matt was struggling with Bryce's decision last weekend. He'd been quiet. Sometimes abrupt. He wasn't sleeping well. She knew it was coming from frustration. So she'd been patient, focusing on her writing to distract herself. She knew he'd work through the surprise his brother had dropped on him eventually. And then they'd figure out where he and she were going.

But his announcement that morning had floored her.

"Matt…" His name came out on an exhale. "You can't be serious. There's no way I can fly to Lake Louise in *Canada* with you. I mean…it's not even in the realm of possibility." How could he not know this? She walked out of the kitchen to where he stood by the window. Sophie was lying at his feet, staring up at him with all her newfound adoration for the man. If only she knew the damage his words had done to Jillie's heart.

Matt's voice was brittle. "You told me you've flown before. You went to Europe! And now you won't even think about it? So you're never going to leave Gallant Lake again? *Ever?*"

"I hadn't thought about it. There hasn't been a need…"

He spun on his heel, slapping his chest with his hand. "*I'm* your need, Jillie. I love you, but it's not fair of you to expect me to just sit in Gallant Lake the rest of my life."

Her spine stiffened at the unexpected attack.

"I beg your pardon? I've never once said you were chained to this town. Or to *me*, for that matter." Her irritation flared. "Don't use your love for me as a weapon, or turn it into some burden." She stood right in front of him, staring up at his hard—no, more like *terrified*—gaze. If anyone could recognize panic, it was Jillie. Her voice softened. "You've known from the very start what my limitations are. Don't you remember our date at the resort? If my anxiety is suddenly a problem…"

He put his hands on her shoulders, his voice heavy with pleading. "The thing is, your limitations are…well, they can be changed. You don't *have* to be this way…"

"I didn't *choose* to be agoraphobic in the first place, Matt. I can't just switch it off. Haven't you learned that yet?" She pulled away from his grip and walked away, unable to think clearly while looking into his eyes. She wrapped her arms around her waist, hugging herself tightly. The thought of walking through an airport, going through Customs, boarding a flight…it was horrifying. Having Matt be the one to suggest it was even more so. "This is me. If you can't accept me as I am, tell me right now, and walk away before we get any deeper."

Matt muttered something she couldn't hear, then tried again. "You're not even trying to change. You're willing to hide in this self-imposed prison…"

She laughed harshly, turning away so he wouldn't see her tears. "This home is hardly a *prison*. Neither is Gallant Lake. I'm not hiding." She ignored the new little voice in her head saying maybe she was. "I'm comfortable here."

"And that's enough? To be *comfortable*?" He

walked up behind her but didn't touch her. "You talk about me not accepting you, but, babe…that goes both ways. I've been following Bryce around the world for years."

She faced him, blinking rapidly. "You just told me I don't *have* to be the way I am. Well, right back atcha." She raised her chin. "Like it or not, you're not Bryce's manager anymore. You don't need to follow him everywhere he goes. In fact, I'm pretty sure he'd rather you didn't."

His jaw tightened. A vein in his neck pulsed in a hard rhythm. "I'm still his brother. I'm not just going to turn my back on him because he's got some hot-shot sports agent now." He huffed out a bitter laugh. "A hotshot agent he met here in freakin' Gallant Lake. Some hotshot, right?"

"Shane Brannigan's firm represents some of the biggest names in sports, and you know it." He wouldn't look her in the eye. She reached out, resting her hand on his forearm. The muscles went taut beneath her fingers. This conversation was about a lot more than Matt and her. He was losing the only identity he'd known as an adult. He was scared. "There's more to you than being Bryce Danzer's big brother. Bryce Danzer's manager. Bryce Danzer's fixer, cleaning up after his misadventures. I told you once that you'd given up your future to raise Bryce, and I admire you for that. But, Matt…" She squeezed his arm until he finally looked at her. "You *did* your job. You've honored your promise to your parents. You raised a good man. And now you get to let him go. You get to be…you."

There was the slightest moment of relaxation in the lines around his eyes. His shoulders relaxed. His jaw unclenched. But it didn't last long. The steeliness returned, defiant and unwilling to let him go. She knew what it was like when your brain didn't want to let go of a belief, and she sighed. They were both stuck in unhealthy patterns. And she had no idea how either one of them would break free.

"I'm still his brother." His voice was almost child-like in its conviction.

"You'll *always* be his brother. That won't change, whether you're his manager or not. In fact, I'm guessing things will be *better* between you without all that business pressure. You do your thing and he'll do his. You just have to figure out what your *thing* is. And where you'll do it." She added that last part in hopes he'd say Gallant Lake.

Matt shook his head, rejecting her logic. "Bryce said he still needed a cheerleader. That's me. I'm the cheerleader." He chewed the inside of his cheek. "It was never my plan to stay in Gallant Lake. This was supposed to be a quiet little pit stop. Great plan, right? Now my whole freakin' life has blown up, and you won't even try to see things my way. So where does that leave us?"

Where, indeed?

"I love you, Matt."

"I know. But…"

She held her hand up in front of his face, her patience wearing thin. "I really need you to stop using that word."

Matt's brow rose. "Love?"

"But." She sighed. "Earlier, you said you love me *but.* Now you say you know I love you, *but.* If you have to qualify the word *love* with a *but* every time, it makes me wonder what love means to you. To us."

"That's not fair."

"I don't have any more experience at falling in love than you do, but I'm pretty sure fairness isn't what defines it." She stepped back. "That makes it sound like a business proposition. Love is an emotion."

"Just like fear."

"And your point?" Didn't he see that he was just as scared as she was?

Matt's jaw ground together again, and he rubbed the back of his neck. "Hell, I don't even know. I'm not in a good head place right now, Jillie. I should go. Bryce's announcement threw me, and I don't want to say anything here that will blow us up any more than we are."

She blew out a long breath.

"My mental limitation is no different than if I had a physical limitation. I know it's not easy to deal with, but if you can't handle who I am, then we have a problem much larger than you having a disagreement with Bryce." She felt a sad certainty that made her heart ache with a pain like none she'd felt before now. "This moment was always coming for us, wasn't it? You need to be on the go. I don't. I can't." She gestured to the ticket in his hand. "And that plane ticket tells me you don't get that."

His eyes narrowed. "If you had a physical limitation that could be eased with treatment, but refused it, then…" He paused, probably realizing he was digging himself a bigger hole. "You know what? Never mind. It's not my place to convince you to seek assistance. To *live* instead of doing all these work-arounds." He tossed the ticket onto a side table. "That piece of paper tells you I wanted you with me. It's a direct flight. I got us in the emergency row, and I bought all three seats so it would just be us. I'd be with you the whole time."

Just the thought of being on a plane, with no control and no escape, made her heart race. The thought of Matt walking away made it break. She put her hand on her chest and closed her eyes, trying to stop the panic attack building in her like a bomb with a very short fuse.

"Jillie?" She heard his voice, but it sounded as if he was talking through a tin can. *Damn it.* She didn't want this to happen *now*. He already thought she was damaged goods with her phobia. Having a flat-out panic attack in front of him wasn't going to make things better. She bit the inside of her cheek hard, trying to distract herself. When she opened her eyes, he was reaching for her. She took another step back, bumping into the window behind her. Sophie appeared at her side, leaning in for support.

"You should leave, Matt." She got just enough air in to say a few words. She looked at the table next to her. "Take the ticket. I'm not going. You knew that when you bought them."

"I was hoping…"

"You got those tickets as an ultimatum." She pulled in a deep breath, doing her best not to show how difficult it was. "As a test."

"No."

"And I failed. Please…just go." Her fingernails were digging deep into her palms, giving her something to focus on other than the ache in her chest. Matt started to argue, then nodded silently and went to the door. He was opening it when she spoke again. "I never said you had to stay here forever. You could have gone to Lake Louise and *come back*. Just because I can't travel doesn't mean *you* can't."

Maybe it was the extra distance between them. Maybe it was because she was standing up for herself. But her panic was receding. Unfortunately, it left only despair behind. "You're looking for someone to be mad at." He raised his head and glowered at her, but she knew she was right. "Just because

I understand doesn't mean I'm willing to be your scapegoat."

"I thought you'd want to be with me."

Tears built up again as she realized the two of them had been carrying very different visions of what life together would look like.

"And I thought you understood my mental health issues."

A gust of wind rattled the door, making him grip the handle more tightly.

"I thought I did, babe. Look, maybe I got ahead of myself with the tickets. But you make it sound like it's *never* going to happen. I don't know how we go forward like that. I don't want to always be saying goodbye to you."

The only sound was Sophie's soft whine as she rested her head on Jillie's thigh and stared up at her with wide, dark eyes full of concern.

Jillie was surprised at the strength of her own voice. "You should go."

He started to argue, then nodded sadly. "The break might give you and me a chance to think things through. Maybe loving each other doesn't mean we actually make *sense* together. Maybe it's not enough." His steel-blue gaze burned her skin. "If that's what we decide—that we're no good for each other—then let's agree right now that it won't be anyone's fault. No scapegoats. Just two people who loved a lot, but…wrong time, wrong place." He opened the door wider. "Goodbye, Jillie."

She stayed upright somehow, listening as he headed down the drive. Once she knew there was no chance he could see her, she sank to the floor and let out a loud, anguished cry. He'd left her. Rejected her. Didn't want her. She buried her face in her hands, ignoring Sophie's attempts to lick her tears away. She screamed in frustration, her cries echoing inside the cabin. Nothing was going to change while he was gone. Neither of them was willing or able to change who they were. This wasn't some "break" they were taking.

This was goodbye.

The drive to the main road felt endless to Matt. It was as if there was a giant bungee cord tied to the bumper of his car, working to pull him back up to the A-frame and into Jillie's arms. He sat at the bottom of the hill for a long time. *Should* he go back? Or was he doing the right thing by giving her space… giving *them* space? He thought of how pale her face had been. The little crack in her voice. The way her hand had fluttered up to cover her heart. She'd told him to leave. He had to honor that. But he didn't have to leave her alone. He pulled his phone out of his pocket, sliding the car into Park.

"What's up, Matt?" Amanda Randall sounded breathless, as if she'd been running.

"Hey…uh…are you busy right now?"

She laughed. "You mean other than chasing a six-year-old up three flights of stairs because she thinks she's wearing shorts to her dance class tonight when it's ten degress outside? No, not busy at all. What do you need?"

"Could you check in on Jillie?"

There was a quick beat of silence before Amanda replied, suddenly all business.

"Why? Where is she? Why can't you check on her?"

"She's home. I just left. We…we had a conversation that didn't go well."

"You mean a fight?"

He shook his head. "Not really. Just a disagreement on some fundamental things."

"That sounds like corporate-speak for *fight*." She spoke to someone else, her words muffled, before returning to the call. "I'll be at her place in ten minutes. How is she?"

"She was calm when I left, but I think that was just on the surface."

"Then why didn't you stay?"

He heard the judgment in her voice and accepted it. It was sinking in now that he may have walked away from everything he'd ever wanted in his life. He'd walked away from Jillie. From a chance at love.

"She told me to leave, Amanda. So I left. I don't want her to be alone."

"Because you love her."

The words hit him like a bullet…straight to the heart.

"She told you that?"

"Please…she didn't have to. We can all see it."

He rubbed his brow with his fingers, feeling a headache coming on that might never go away. He could hear a car door opening on the other end of the call, and an echo as it switched to the speaker in Amanda's car. He sighed, putting his own car in Drive and pulling out onto the main road.

"I *do* love her. But that may not be enough to overcome our differences…"

Amanda's sharp laugh surprised him.

"Oh, you sweet, sweet summer child. Of course love is enough, if you let it be."

"I have no idea what that means."

"You're a smart guy. You'll figure it out. Unless you're *willing* to let her go, in which case you're not so smart after all."

"We're taking a break to think things through. I'm flying up to Lake Louise to join Bryce and Shane at a ski event there." The thought of sitting next to those two empty seats on the plane made him feel hollow inside.

"You're *leaving Gallant Lake*? Right after a fight?"

He groaned. "I told you it wasn't a fight. We

didn't yell. There wasn't any name-calling. It was just an...emotional discussion."

"And you're leaving town right afterward."

His fingers gripped the steering wheel so tight his knuckles turned white.

"What *is* this place—Hotel California? Now that I'm here I can never leave? I have a responsibility to my brother, and his life takes him around the globe. It's been *my* life for over ten years now, and I don't see that changing." Jillie kept trying to tell him it had already changed, but he couldn't forget standing at his parents' graves, vowing to take care of Bryce. That vow didn't have an expiration date.

"If you and Jillie are truly in love with each other, your life has already changed, sweetie." She paused. "Did you say Shane Brannigan was going to be in Canada with Bryce?"

"He's Bryce's new manager, so he'd better be." He rolled his eyes at himself. "Sorry, I know he's your cousin's husband. I'm still adjusting to the whole thing."

"It's fine. Shane's good people, but it's natural for you to be cautious." He was pretty sure she was laughing again. "Why don't you ask him about how he and Mel got together, and what happened when he left Gallant Lake."

"Left? Didn't they just build that new house? And Mel owns a business here." Matt turned down the small road to his rental.

"Well, sure...*now*. There was a time when Shane couldn't wait to shake this place off his shoes and hit the big time. Just ask him about it." She paused. "I'm turning into Jillie's now. Don't worry about her, okay? She's stronger than she seems."

"Let me know she's all right."

"I will. And, Matt?"

"Yeah?"

"You'll never forgive yourself if you let her go."

The small house was too quiet with Bryce gone. Matt paced the floors. It was over an hour before Amanda texted that Jillie was okay. He asked for more details, but all she'd say was Jillie would be fine. That's what he was afraid of—that she'd be fine without him. And that he wouldn't be fine at all.

He eventually plunked himself down on the sofa and turned on an old Jason Bourne movie. He and Bryce used to watch these in hotel rooms all the time, joking that there was always a Bourne movie playing somewhere in the world. The familiarity helped him unwind enough to doze off before the movie was over.

He woke up a little after dawn, one leg hanging off the sofa, his head on the arm, the pillow on the floor. His neck ached from the awkward position, but he was able to stretch it out. He needed to get on the road if he was going to be at the airport on time. A shower helped, and he tossed some clothes and his kit into a duffel bag. He checked with Gary at the ski lodge and it seemed like everything would be under control for a few days without him. He checked the time, and called Jillie. Just to make sure she was okay. Just to hear her voice. He was surprised when Amanda Randall answered, speaking softly.

"Matt? Didn't you say you were leaving this morning?"

"Amanda? Where's Jillie? What happened?"

Amanda chuckled, speaking a little louder now. "Jillie's still sleeping. I stayed overnight, just to keep her company."

Jillie never slept this late. Even if she wanted to, Sophie would have woken her. Amanda could let the dog out, but why would she have stayed all night?

"What happened?"

"Hang on…" He heard a door open and close. "Okay, I'm outside. What happened is some *idiot* suggested she walk through a crowded New York City airport to catch a flight." His eyes closed tightly. That really had been a stupid idea. Amanda didn't wait for his reaction. "Jillie's going to be fine. Broken hearts mend eventually."

"I'm coming over." He grabbed his keys off the counter and his jacket from the wall hook. "I need to see her with my own eyes."

"No, Matt. There's no sense starting everything up again until you two have figured out where your heads are at."

He'd bungled things so badly. He jammed his fingers through his hair, clenching it tight in frustration. He didn't want to leave Gallant Lake. But he wasn't sure this was where he was supposed to be.

"I could stay." He should stay.

"Isn't Bryce expecting you?"

He silently swore to himself.

"How am I supposed to balance it all? Bryce. Jillie. I'll always be saying goodbye to one or the other."

There was a long beat of silence before Amanda answered.

"You'll also always be saying hello to one or the other."

Chapter Thirteen

The poison was worming its way toward her heart now. She could feel it burning through her veins. She welcomed it. She looked across the mountaintop to Robbie's body. So very still. Had they won? Her eyes fell closed. Did winning matter if they'd paid so high a price?

"Girl, you are one depressing pile of self-pity right now."

Mackenzie Adams looked across the table at Jillie, who had no argument to offer in return. Her other friends nodded in unison as they sat in the solarium at Halcyon. The snow was glistening outside the semicircular, glass-enclosed room. It was pretty, but it wasn't helping her mood any. Snow made her think of the mountain. The mountain made her think of Matt. And Matt had been gone for a week.

Nora refilled everyone's wineglasses, except for Mel Brannigan, who was drinking seltzer. As Nora set down the wine bottle, she looked over at Jillie.

"What can we do to help, sweetie?"

Jillie tried and failed to smile. "Anyone have a magic wand to fix my brain?"

Silence fell. Not even the clink of glass or silverware. It was Amanda who spoke first.

"There is *nothing* wrong with your brain."

"Hear, hear." Mel raised her glass. "You are a strong, independent woman. A *successful* woman. A *smart* woman."

Mack's eyebrow arched high. "That's all true, but it doesn't change the fact that you're also a depressing pile of self-pity."

Jillie finally laughed a little at that. Her laughter seemed to ease the tension in the room. This gathering had been Nora's idea. A ladies' lunch to get Jillie away from the mountain. She hadn't wanted to come, of course, but Nora had suggested it to her five minutes after her agent had ordered her to step away from the book and "get the hell out of that house." Nia had clearly ratted her out to Lisa after she'd told her assistant that she felt like a well that had run dry. Getting words on the page felt like slogging through quicksand this past week. She looked around the table, where her Gallant Lake friends were watching her hopefully. Would her laughter continue? Was she better? Was she *fixed*?

"I'm not *trying* to be a depressing pile of self-pity. And I'm not even sure it's self-pity, not necessarily. It's…" She stared up at the ceiling, searching for words. "I'm…lonely."

Mack gestured around the table. "How can you be lonely sitting with this group of fabulous women?"

Amanda reached out and placed her hand over Jillie's. "She's lonely for one particular person, and he's not here right now."

Nora frowned. "You haven't heard from him at all?"

Jillie shrugged. "A couple texts. A couple voice-mails." She shouldn't have shared that last bit. Nora pounced right away.

"Why voicemails? Why didn't you answer his calls?"

"There's nothing to say to him, is there? He left."

Amanda's eyes narrowed. "He said you *told* him to leave."

"Sure, I told him to leave the house. That day. That conversation." She blinked. "I didn't want him to *leave*-leave. I don't think…" She rushed on. "I mean, if he can't accept that I'm not going globe-trotting with him, what's the point? I don't need to hear about Lake Louise and all his adventures, knowing that he wants me to be *with* him there. It'll just make me feel even worse. It'll make *him* feel worse." She was aware that her voice was rising, but she couldn't seem to stop. "He's not going to want to sit around here with me when there's a whole… a whole *world* out there that he loves being part of! He and I make no sense. None at all. He told me I *hide* behind my fears. Can you imagine? I *hide*! Like I'd choose this."

Mack sat back, muttering something. Mel elbowed her hard, but everyone suddenly looked uncomfortable. Jillie scowled at them.

"If you have something to say, just say it."

Amanda pursed her lips tightly, staring at the table. Jillie finally got it.

"Oh, my God. You all think he's right."

Amanda shook her head firmly, blond waves brushing back and forth over her shoulders. "No, no, no. Not…not really. But, Jillie, from one therapy patient to another, there *are* things we can do to make things better. When's the last time you talked to anyone?"

"Someone professional, you mean?" Jillie frowned. How long *had* it been?

Amanda pushed her wineglass away. "I have definitely had too much wine. That question was wildly inappropriate and none of my business. Forget I said anything."

Nora quickly moved the conversation away from

Jillie's therapy status and on to the fascinating topic of how excited she was to find ethically harvested coffee beans from Costa Rica to brew in the shop. Mel, Mack and Amanda acted *very* excited at the news. Jillie knew it was all an act for her benefit, but she was okay with that. It allowed her to sit quietly with her own thoughts while they talked. Her thoughts were far less comforting than she would have liked.

Matt *had* called. Twice. He'd left the first voicemail the day after he left, and it had been stilted and uncertain. She'd stared at his number on the screen when it rang, but didn't answer. What if he said goodbye for good?

Uh...yeah...just wanted you to know I made it here... It's colder than hell... Shane got Bryce into the announcer's booth for an interview, which I would never have pulled off... Uh... I miss you, babe. I'm sorry... God, I'm so sorry. I was an idiot. Call me back, Jillie. Please.

She hadn't called back. She had no idea what to say. The idea of dialing the phone made her break out in a chilly sweat. He'd waited another day before calling again. She legitimately missed that one. She'd fallen asleep on the sofa after a near-sleepless night, and never heard the phone. This message was a bit more organized. And more resigned.

Jillie... Please don't end us all by yourself before we had a chance to begin. I'm not going to harass

you with calls you clearly don't want, but we have
to talk when I get back. I don't know what the an-
swer is, but there has to be one. I love you, Jillie.

After that it was just texts. One per day. He didn't
plead in his texts. He didn't even ask questions, as if
he knew she wasn't going to reply. He told her what
the days were like. He and Bryce had done some
"gentle" skiing away from reporters one afternoon.
Bryce's interview had gone so well that they asked
him to come back as a guest commentator. Other
than the occasional accidental curse word on air,
he was doing well. Matt said he and Shane had had
some "good talks," but he never said what they were
about. He talked about the weather—cold—and the
food—delicious. He told her Gary was doing a great
job with the ski resort. And he let her know when
his return flight was arriving that weekend.

She'd looked forward to the texts every night, but
at the same time they made her sad. A relationship
couldn't survive on text messages. And she'd never
be able to travel with him. She smiled at whatever
her friends were laughing about. Mel had been talking, so it was probably a funny story about baby
Patrick.

Except… Jillie *had* traveled before. Before she let
her world shrink to only what made her comfortable.
An international flight might be a step too far right
now, but maybe she could try something…smaller.
Easier. With some help.

* * *

"Seriously, Bryce." Matt shook his head. "You could fall into a pile of cow dung and come up smelling like a rose."

His brother raised his beer to meet his toast. The bar was packed with skiers and fans, and several women weren't even trying to be discreet in their attempts to capture Bryce on their phones.

Shane laughed and clinked his beer against theirs in the center of the small corner table. "Hey, the kid earned this job fair and square."

Matt shook his head. "I'm not denying that, although he had a lot of help from his new agent." Matt clinked his glass against Shane's. "It's just…this has been the story of his life. Thrown off the team? No problem. He runs the race of his life and he's back on. Gets caught drinking at three in the morning the night before a race…when he's *sixteen*? No problem. He wins the slalom the next morning and suddenly no one cares. Starts a fight in the chute right before the world championships? Everyone covers for him, even the guy he gave a black eye to. Breaks his goddamn leg in Italy being a hot dog and has to miss an entire season? No problem—he's got himself a job sitting in the commentator's booth." Matt gestured around the bar, where phones were still pointed their way. "And now he's skiing's sweetheart again."

Bryce laughed before taking another swig of beer. You could almost hear the young women swooning at the tables around them. "I can't help it if I'm a natural. Oh, hey—one of the guys I used to train with just came in." He stood and plunked his empty mug on the table. "See you old dudes later."

Shane clutched his chest as if he'd been shot. "Ow, that hurt!" He was clowning, but he caught Bryce's arm before he walked away. "Remember our deal."

Bryce rolled his eyes, but his reply was low and serious. "I had one beer, Pops. I'm allowed one more, and the alarm is set on my phone. I'll turn into a boring little pumpkin at midnight and go up to my room. Alone." He winked in Matt's direction. "Probably. Shane promised he'd dump my ass if I got in trouble during an event or on the job."

Shane nodded. "Yup. We made a deal that *during* events Bryce absolutely has to behave himself. Like a choir boy."

Matt nodded toward the empty beer glass on the table. "Not exactly a choir boy."

Shane gave Bryce a shove away from the table. "We compromised on the definition, but not on the enforcement." Bryce waved goodbye and headed off toward the bar. Shane turned back to Matt. "I don't usually compromise with my clients, but damn that kid is persuasive. He'd make a great agent someday."

"I don't know…sounds like you've got him lined up to be a sports announcer."

"He's a natural. He knows everyone in skiing and

snowboarding, even outside his areas of competition. He's cocky but self-deprecating at the same time, with a great sense of humor. And the camera loves the kid." Shane shrugged. "I want him to be competing, of course, but when he's not on the slopes, I think the network might be interested."

"That's a deal I never could have made for him. Or the sportswear sponsorship."

"It was good timing. I knew the company was looking for a younger, fresher spokesperson. Your brother's about as young and fresh as they get." Shane grinned. "And don't forget—this is what I do for a living. You did a great job keeping Bryce out of *real* trouble when you were his manager. You knew when to take him out of the limelight, and that's a valuable skill to have." Shane waved at a server and gestured for two more beers. "You kept his name clean enough that sponsors aren't afraid of him. I might offer *you* a job."

Matt started to laugh, until he realized Shane was serious. Shane nodded.

"Yes, really. Our agency manages as well as represents, and we do seem to attract younger stars who have…image issues…with the public. You've got the management part down pat. And my partner and I can do the money-making part." He paid the server and handed Matt a glass. "You'll probably have your hands full with the ski slope, but if you want to do some part-time consulting or troubleshooting, let me know. How's Gary doing with the place this week?"

"Good, I guess. Dan and Blake have both been up there to check on things, and their reports line up with Gary's. Busy enough to keep the lights on, and customers seem happy. Making snow every night, and the base is up to eighteen inches on some slopes." He sipped his beer. "Looks like we're going to land that high school mini-event you sent our way. Their original venue hasn't reopened since the pandemic. It's going to be intense to pull it together that fast, but we'll do our best."

"Let me know the dates," Shane said. "I've got Bryce lined up to make an appearance in Davos, but he could hop back to the States between that and the Worlds in Italy and make an appearance. I'll see if we can line up some press for it, which would make Bryce look good, and wouldn't hurt your bottom line, either. Lord knows Gallant Lake could use the winter tourism. My wife's boutique is still recovering from the pandemic shutdown."

Matt had walked into Mel Brannigan's Five and Design boutique one day by accident. He was on his phone and walking toward the liquor store but went in the wrong door. The place was nice—a former general store converted to women's clothing and accessories. Mel had greeted him warmly and shown him around, her infant son propped on her hip. The second floor was a bridal salon, and she said her office was on the third floor. An office she shared with Shane. Matt remembered Amanda's advice to him last week.

"Someone suggested I ask you about when you left Gallant Lake."

Shane barked out a loud laugh, turning heads around them.

"Let me guess—it was one of Mel's cousins. They will never let me live that down. But I deserve the roasting. I nearly chased the wrong dream." His brows lowered. "Actually, I *did* chase the wrong one, at least for a while."

Shane told Matt how much he'd scoffed at Gallant Lake when he'd first arrived there with a young golfing client, trying to keep her out of the limelight. Very similar to Matt's plan for Bryce, actually. That was when he'd met Melanie Lowery, formerly known as supermodel Mellie Low. They'd had their share of disagreements, but it didn't stop them from falling in love.

There was just one problem. Mel had no intention of leaving Gallant Lake. After a life of globe-hopping as a model, she'd ended up addicted to pills and alcohol. Her continued recovery depended on being someplace peaceful and supportive. That place for her was Gallant Lake. When Shane got the job offer he'd been dreaming of, at the largest talent agency in the country, he'd assumed Mel would come to LA with him. Because they loved each other.

"The day I told her about the job—" Shane stared hard into his glass "—was the day she told me she'd bought that run-down old shop on Main Street. When I suggested she give up her dream for mine, she made it clear that wasn't going to happen. Los Angeles represented everything she was trying to escape." He gave Matt a somber look. "And she called me out on the misguided motivation for my life choices and what it was going to do to me."

"But you left, anyway?"

"Yup. Just stamp the word *dumbass* on my forehead. I went to LA, got the corner office and the fancy title I'd vowed I'd have someday. I thought maybe Mel would follow me. But she knew what she needed, and it was in Gallant Lake. Whether I was there or not." He took a sip of beer and his mouth slid into a crooked grin. "Turns out what *I* needed was *her*, so I came back. I had to grovel a little. We both had to compromise. We loved each other, so we worked it out." His smile deepened. "And I'm guessing you're asking me about this because of our mutual author friend on Watcher Mountain?"

Matt nodded. "But Mel still travels with you once in a while, right? Weren't you two in London for the holidays?"

"Mel avoids stressful situations, but her situation is not as extreme as Jillie's. She's in a twelve-step program, has a great sponsor and even acts as a sponsor for another young woman in town. She'll make the occasional trip with me, but it's usually for vacation, not work. We have our own careers and we manage them separately from each other. But our marriage and our family is handled as a complete partnership."

"Yet you're here and she's at home alone."

"Yup. Your point?" Shane cocked a brow.

"Come on," Matt protested. "It can't be easy. Being in love doesn't make it easy…"

Shane's laughter rang out again. "Hoo-boy. No, being in love doesn't make many things easy. Falling? That's easy. Staying? Well, in relationships like ours, it takes a lot of communication and zero assumptions. Set expectations. Assume nothing." He sat back and held up his phone. "Technology helps. We talk a couple times a day, and we're constantly texting." He chuckled and turned the phone around. "Look what she sent me this afternoon."

It was a video of Mel and the baby playing in the snow. The little boy was laughing, and Mel was, too. They were on a plastic sled, sliding down a modest hill together toward the frozen lake. It was only a few seconds long, but judging from Shane's expression, it had made his day. Could Matt and Jillie do something like this? Would it work if he was going to Bryce's events and she wasn't? Could he be happy with Gallant Lake as a home base?

He thought about what real estate agent Brittany Doyle had discussed with him—going into partnership and flipping properties in the area. With the resort expanding into vacation condos this summer and adding a major tournament to the resort's golf course, housing was bound to be in demand. Brittany was interested in flipping some of the storefronts in town, too, in order to attract new businesses to Main Street. It wasn't like he wouldn't have work to do in Gallant Lake if he wanted it. Along with the ski lodge. Was that what he wanted? Was that what Jillie wanted? She hadn't returned his calls. She hadn't responded to his clumsy texts. She hadn't told him to take a hike, either.

This week in Canada had proved that there was only one thing that mattered. He needed to have Jillie in his life. And if that meant she never left Gallant Lake, then they'd have to find a way to make that work. She was worth it. *They* were worth it.

Chapter Fourteen

"I told you to let me go." Monica glared at Tiesha, furious to wake and discover she was still alive. Still had battles to fight. Without Robbie. As if reading her mind, Tiesha smiled, leaning over to whisper the words, "He lives. He needs your healing touch, but he lives."

Matt had been back in Gallant Lake for a week. Jillie knew that because everyone had seen and/or talked to him. Everyone but her. Oh, he'd checked in with texts every day. He was so very busy getting ready for the winter break week coming up. They'd done a lot of promo for the junior Alpine event, he explained. It was very important. Bryce would be there. The press would be there. Crowds would be there. So important. So busy.

The *crowds* part should have freaked her out. But she was much more concerned with why Matt was avoiding her. It felt as if he'd firmly moved her into the *friendly neighbor zone.* Maybe he was presenting some unspoken ultimatum—if she wanted him, she'd have to go after him.

A flutter of tension tightened her chest. She looked around the living room and started doing inventory, as her new therapist had taught her. Blue lamp. Cherry table. Brown leather sofa with three cushions. Red-and-blue Oriental rug. Dark red leather wingback chair. Another red leather wingback chair. Photo of her on a horse. She took a deep breath, and felt better. The trick was working. Especially when combined with the new medication she was taking for her anxiety. Dr. Jackson assured her on their last video call that the medication would probably be temporary. That once Jillie learned new coping mechanisms and pushed herself outside her comfort zone—and survived—things would become easier.

Back to Matt. *What was he up to?* And why did all of her friends…her friends *long* before Matt showed up…seem to be conspiring with him somehow? Or at the very least, gaslighting her. So much talk about the "exciting" ski competition.

Had she heard that some of the top junior skiers in the country would be in town? *So exciting!* Amanda was raving about how busy the Gallant Lake Resort was. Nora was stocking up on that Costa Rican coffee. Mel was rushing an order of genuine Irish sweaters for the boutique. Wasn't it *exciting*? Mack had moved the top-shelf liquor to the front of the store, hoping some of the wealthier ski fans would want to pick up some of the good stuff to take back to their rooms. She told Jillie that Dan had coordinated additional traffic assistance from the state troopers. It would be an *exciting* weekend!

They weren't being cruel about it. It didn't feel like taunting or teasing. They were all checking in on her regularly, making sure she was okay. Making sure she had what she needed. And she did… everything except Matt. And he was right next door. Being busy. Exciting, right?

She pulled on her down jacket, wool cap and warmest boots before taking Sophie for a walk. They'd had an extended cold snap, and it was supposed to last right into next week. More snow in the forecast, too. Perfect ski weather. Anytime she'd stepped outside lately, she'd heard the snowmaking machines. It seemed they were running around the clock this week. Getting ready for that *exciting* event.

She was sticking to one or two paths these days, so she could keep them packed down and manageable to walk. There was a lot of hammering coming from near the slopes as she and Sophie headed up Watcher Mountain. She'd heard that yesterday, too. Part of the ski course? A judges' stand? Maybe the starting gates? Except it sounded so close. As if it was directly across from Jillie's house. She looked at the ten inches of soft, new snow on the ground and then at her boots. They were tall enough to keep her dry, and curiosity got the best of her. She whistled to Sophie and headed through the trees.

It wasn't long before she realized what was being built. A *fence*. A tall, sturdy wooden fence along the edge of her property. Jillie stood in stunned silence. The privacy would be nice. But it felt a little… insulting. Like a barricade. As if Matt was walling her off. Sophie sat in the snow and watched the people skiing on the slopes, but Jillie paid them no mind as she stepped out to look at the fence.

The fence posts ran quite a way up the mountain, and down beyond the lodge's parking lot. There was a team of four workers nailing the wood panels to the posts. They had a small snowblower with them, which they used to clear down to the grass before adding the panels. This was no temporary fence. The four-by-four posts had cemented bases. They must have started work on it days ago, but she hadn't heard anything until the hammering began.

"Hey, stranger!" Bryce had been skiing down the slope, but turned and stopped a few feet away with a playful spray of snow. Sophie leaped up and ran to greet him. He laughed and roughhoused with her for a minute.

"Bryce! I didn't know you were back already! How was Italy?"

"Hectic." His face twisted a little. "And weird. I was there as a commentator, not a competitor, but people seemed to like it, so…"

"I saw you on television—you did a *great* job! You're a natural." She gestured toward his skis. "I bet you're happy to be doing this again."

"Yeah, the doc cleared me for whatever he thinks *normal* skiing is for me." Bryce winked. "Which means I snuck out on the slopes in Italy after the competitions were done. Not racing, but it felt great to be back on a slalom course again. I met up with one of the US coaches, and he said I looked good, considering. I'll start training in earnest in a few weeks." He gestured toward the fence. "What do you think?"

"I…I don't know *what* to think. Why is he doing this?"

Bryce's eyes went wide. "For *you.*" When she didn't answer, he continued. "There will be a fair number of people here next week. He didn't want anyone wandering into your woods, by accident or on purpose. The fence makes it clear this is off-limits, and it's far enough off the main slope so that it's not a hazard."

Off-limits. Was that what Matt thought of her these days?

"Jillie? You okay?"

She smiled. "Yeah. Fine. How's Matt doing? I hear he's busy."

"You haven't talked to him?" Bryce frowned. "What's going on with you two?"

"That's the million-dollar question, I'm afraid." Sophie came to lean against her, and Jillie looked down, scratching the dog's ears absently. "We had a…a falling out, I guess. He wanted me to go to Lake Louise with him, which just wasn't possible. He was upset. I was upset. Things were said. We decided to take a break…but we didn't really define what that meant or how long it might last." She looked back to Bryce. "He's kept me posted on how busy he is, so I get it."

"So…you *have* talked?"

"He texts."

Bryce stared. "And you *answer* those texts?"

"Well…no. He doesn't ask for responses of any kind. He just sends daily news bulletins. Like he did when you guys were in Canada."

"Let me get this straight. My brother has been texting you *daily* for two weeks, and you haven't responded *once*?"

Her mouth dropped open, but she didn't know what to say. They stared at each other in silence, before Bryce shook his head with a low laugh.

"I've been on Matt's case for days about how he's handling this, but it's clear now that it really does take two to tango. You guys are seriously dysfunctional, and you need to figure your sh…" He hesitated. "Your *stuff* out. I'm no relationship expert, but I'm pretty sure that means actual communication. He didn't tell you about the fence?"

She shook her head.

"And did he tell you what he did in the lodge? Adding shutters to all the new windows facing your place, so they can be closed up tight to block the view? Or that he's *not* coming to the Worlds next month because he needs to talk to Brittany Doyle about some old houses she wants to flip?"

She shook her head again, but her heart began to warm at the reason he might be doing these things.

"Did he tell you…?" He straightened and shuffled his skis around to point back toward the slope. "You know what? Never mind. He's probably thinking he's going to surprise you with some grand gesture or something, but…" Bryce stopped abruptly, then closed his eyes tightly. "Oh, damn. He probably *is* doing that, and I blew it."

"No! I'm the one who found the fence."

"But you *didn't* know about the other things, like the job or…oh, *shut up*, Bryce!" He slapped the side of his head with the palm of his hand. "Look…act surprised, okay? Whatever it is he has planned…act surprised." He looked around, but no one seemed to be paying any attention to them at the edge of the woods. "And we never had this conversation, got it?"

She laughed—her first real laugh in two weeks—and nodded.

"Got it. And, Bryce? I'm really happy that you're back on skis and able to travel the circuit with your friends." She couldn't resist adding a bit of self-pity. "I'm sure Matt enjoys all the travel, too."

"Now that he approves of my new manager, I think Matt will be backing off on the traveling." He gave her a pointed look. "A *lot*. Oh, in case you're wondering, see that section right there?" He gestured a few yards down the mountain. "That's where the gate's going."

With a swish of snow, he was gone, flying down the slope toward the lodge. She turned to look at where the gate was going to be. There was a big difference between a fence, and a fence with a gate.

She dug her phone out of her pocket as she and Sophie headed back to her house, recalling something that Mack had said. Jillie had ignored it at the time, but now it was tapping at her brain. Mack Adams answered on the first ring.

"Hi, girlfriend!" She sounded out of breath. "I'm finishing up the new window display with all the stuff skiers like to fill their flasks with. Schnapps. Fireball. Cognac. Irish whiskey. I figure if Mel's displaying all those Irish sweaters in *her* windows, I'd better tag along, right? So what's up?"

"Didn't you say something the other day about Dan telling you that Matt and Bryce were going to Lake Placid?" Dead silence. "Mack? Are you there?"

"Why do you want to know about Lake Placid?"

Jillie kicked at a clump of snow and Sophie chased after it. "Why did you *tell* me about Lake Placid if you didn't want me to know about it?"

Mack chuckled. "O-kay. Bryce is going to an event at Whiteface Mountain in a few weeks. It's a big winter sports competition for university teams, and his clothing sponsor wants him there showing off their latest winter wear. Mel said Shane arranged for Bryce to ski down the slopes like a flagbearer or something before the big race, wearing his gold medal." She hesitated. "I'm not sure if Matt is going or not."

Jillie smiled, remembering the weekend she spent in Lake Placid ten years ago. "Oh, he's going. Thanks, Mack. I need to give Shane Brannigan a call."

Chapter Fifteen

The resistance fighters stood in awe as the Shadows rolled back from Stoneroot Mountain. The shadows they'd created. It turned out the monsters were their own fears, manifested through an ancient spell. Once Monica trusted the Wise One enough to learn that, they'd all worked together. Conquering their fears. Bringing peace. It hadn't been easy. There was still danger lurking. But they knew how to fight it now.

Matt wasn't sure when he'd ever been more exhausted. The junior event at Gallant Lake Ski Resort had been a smashing success, considering how last-minute it was. Bryce's name was a big part of that success. Now that people outside Gallant Lake knew Bryce was involved with the lodge, Matt had a feeling they'd be seeing a lot more business. And that was good news for everyone.

As if to confirm, Dan Adams, parked on a bar stool next to Matt in the nearly empty lodge, slid his phone into his pocket with a wide grin.

"Mack said this was one of her best weekends ever for business. That seems to be a universal opinion on Main Street. Nora said she almost ran out of coffee. Mel Brannigan said she *did* sell out of sweaters and hats. Even Asher got some business out of it—not just small stuff but two or three custom-furniture orders to build. Nate said the hardware store was wall-to-wall people once word got out about that parrot of his."

Hank the Foul-mouthed Parrot was well-known in town, although Nate tried to keep the bird's cursing to a minimum. Those plans went out the window once all the teens in town discovered that if they said just one blue word, Hank would go off on a rant. A couple of videos had already gone viral. Bad for Nate's training efforts with Hank, but good for Nate's bottom line. His fiancée, Brittany, suggested they start selling T-shirts and other items featuring Hank, and as much as Nate protested how "tacky" that would be, they'd sold out of T-shirts that week. Dan slapped Matt on the shoulder as he stood.

"You did good, man. If anyone had told me a year ago that this old place would be *open*, much less help put Gallant Lake on the map for winter vacations, I'd have given them a breathalyzer test. But you pulled it off."

Matt shook his head, and the effort was almost too much for him. He couldn't remember the last time he'd slept. "Don't think I've ever been this tired. I need to lock up and get my ass home to bed."

Dan replied with a distracted "Mmm-hmm. Maybe you should stay here a while longer. You're probably too tired to drive."

"It's five miles to the rental house. And it's all downhill. I'll be fine, Mr. Police Chief, sir."

Dan glanced at his watch. That was the third time he'd done that in the past half hour or so. His phone buzzed again, and he turned away from Matt to look at it. When he turned back, he had a big grin on his face.

"I gotta head out. I'll talk to you tomorrow." Dan seemed in a hurry all of a sudden. "You might want to hang out here and have a cup of coffee so your head's clear. You're going to need it."

And he was gone. After an hour of hanging out over a beer once Matt had closed up, Dan hadn't seemed in any kind of hurry. At least not until that last text came through. He stretched, staring at what looked like tar in the bottom of the coffeepot. Dan probably got a booty call invitation from Mack. Or maybe his daughter had needed something. Matt poured black coffee into a mug and sipped it, cringing at the bitterness. That would wake him up long enough to get to the house. In the morning, he was meeting with Brittany Doyle about their plans to flip properties together. She wanted to start with the old bakery, saying the town needed someone to come in and reopen it, and that wouldn't happen the way it looked now.

Once they toured the place and set a budget, she was going to show him the apartment over the former bakery. The vacation rental was nearing the end of his lease, and he couldn't assume Jillie would welcome him into her home with open arms. He wasn't sure she'd welcome him at all, but he had to try. He just needed to get his plans lined up. The fence was done. The shutters were up. He'd walled off one side of the rooftop deck. He wanted her to see how serious he was about giving her what she needed.

He realized he hadn't texted yet tonight. He finished drinking the coffee—*ew*—and pulled his phone out of his pocket. She'd yet to answer his texts, but he could see she was opening every one he sent. And she hadn't blocked him yet, which gave him hope.

Just drank the gross stuff that's been congealing at the bottom of the coffeepot all day. That's how

tired I am. Heading home, but wow, what a weekend. Everyone seems happy.

He stared like he always did, hoping this would
be the time she answered. No floating dots appeared.
He sighed. Once he got some rest and had some work
lined up here in town, he'd go to Jillie and plead his
case. But not tonight. Even the worst coffee in the
world wasn't going to be able to keep him awake
for long. He couldn't resist sending one more text.

I miss you, babe.

Still nothing. It wasn't until he was sliding the
phone back into his pocket that a ripple of awareness
went through him. Whether he'd heard something
or just felt a presence, he knew he wasn't alone. The
surge of adrenaline did far more than the coffee had
to make him alert. Did he need a weapon? Did he
have one within easy reach?

"I miss you, too."

He was hallucinating, probably from the exhaustion. He was hearing things. Hearing *Jillie*. His brain
was torturing him. He slowly turned, knowing the
room would be empty.

Except it wasn't.

Jillie stood there, just inside the door. Sophie was
at her side, watching him with cautious interest. Jillie was bundled in a puffy yellow jacket and fur-

topped snow boots, and was tugging off a yellow knit hat when he turned. Her dark hair fell like satin on her shoulders. Her dark eyes were wide, focused only on him. Jillie. Was here. In the ski lodge. His breath came out long and slow. She was *here*.

And she said she'd missed him. Should he go to her? Should he stay where he was? He wanted to hold her so badly. He didn't move. He didn't speak. Which she found amusing. Her mouth slanted up into a crooked grin.

"Nothing to say?"

"I… Jillie… What…what are you doing here? How…?"

"Dan made sure you'd be here alone with an un-locked door. I drove over, because the snow is a lit-tle deep and I wasn't sure I'd be able to get through the gate."

"You know about the gate." He was stating the obvious. Had she been watching the fence going up? Had she heard it? "Did the hammering disturb your writing? I'm sorry…"

She shook her head, her smile deepening. "It didn't disturb me, although I was curious about why you'd do something like that."

"The gate?"

"The fence."

"To protect you. I didn't want anyone getting nosy about who or what was beyond those trees."

"And the gate?"

His heart and lungs were beginning to function normally again, which helped his brain tremendously. He managed a crooked smile of his own.

"The gate is for *my* protection." Her brows lowered in confusion, so he explained. "There is no way I'd ever be able to put a wall between us that I couldn't get through somehow."

Silence stretched between them, but there was nothing negative about it. He felt at ease for the first time in weeks. And damned if *Jillie* didn't seem relaxed. Inside the ski lodge she'd never visited. She hadn't moved more than a step or two from the door. And now that he studied her more closely, he noticed her gaze flicker around the mostly dark space at regular intervals, checking her safety. This was her. Her insecurity. Her phobias. Her anxiety. He cleared his throat.

"I'm so proud of you for having the strength to do this. Shocked. And proud. If you don't want to be here, it's okay. We can go anywhere you…"

"No." Her voice was firm. "I'm okay here. It's just you and I." She glanced around. "Right?"

"Yeah, babe. Just you and I." He took a step toward her. "And your hellhound." As if Sophie knew she was being discussed, her butt started wiggling as her tail wagged. He took another step. "Is this… Can I…?" Jillie nodded. She was still glued to her spot inside the door. The closer he got, the more he recognized the tension humming just under her skin. This wasn't as easy for her as she was trying to make it look. "Jillie…" He stopped in front of her. He wanted so badly to touch her. "I have so much to say. I don't even know where to begin…"

"You left me." It wasn't as much an accusation as a statement. He nodded.

"You told me to leave."

She nodded in return, and he slowly smiled. "So now that we have that sorted, let me start with this— I love you, Jillie Coleman. I was an idiot to ever make you doubt that, or to think it wasn't enough. You don't have to change one thing for me. Nothing at all. I don't want you to. You're perfect the way you are."

She snorted at that. "Far from perfect. I'm a mess."

"Not a mess." He reached out and took her hands in his. "You have anxiety. You have agoraphobia. That's all part of the Jillie package. It's…" He fumbled for words. "It's *part* of you, but it doesn't *define* you. And it sure as hell doesn't define *us*."

She looked up at him with shimmering dark eyes. "Is there still an *us*?"

"God, I hope so." He squeezed her fingers. "I hope I haven't blown it. I…I wanted to give you space. I'd pushed so hard before the trip. I was a selfish jerk. And I'm sorry. You didn't answer my calls, but then you didn't block my texts, so I was holding out hope that we were still okay. Battered, but okay. I needed that hope." He looked around the lodge. "I didn't know what to do, and we had this event to plan for. Maybe it's selfish again—you may find that's *my* thing—but I thought if I waited until after this weekend, things would be calmer and I'd be able to think of the right things to say." He chuckled. "Except now it's over and you're here and all I can think to say is that I love you."

Jillie smiled. "A few weeks ago you weren't sure if love was enough."

"I'm sure now. Very sure. I've already told Bryce he'll only see me at a couple of the biggest races next year. I can watch him on television or online. I'm staying here."

She drew in a sharp breath, then shook her head. "You've never stayed anywhere for long. Do you really think you can…?"

Matt tugged gently, pulling her into his embrace, where she belonged. She wrapped her arms tightly around his waist, resting her head on his shoulder. Sophie laid down on the floor with a bored sigh. He felt whole again. Complete. Content. Loved. He kissed her hair, rubbing his cheek against her scalp.

"I can do anything for you. If this is the place you have to be, then it's the place *I* have to be, too. I've got the lodge, and I'm going into partnership with Brittany Doyle to flip some properties. I've got work, I've got you and I really don't care if I ever leave." It was true. He could stand like this forever, holding her tight. She shook her head, still close but wiggling to fish in her jacket pocket for something.

"I don't want you chained to Gallant Lake. *I* don't want to be chained to Gallant Lake. You were right about me hiding here. I've got a new therapist and…" She pulled what looked like a folded ticket of some sort out of her pocket and handed it to him. "I'm trying new things. Because of you."

Baffled, he took the ticket and opened it behind her back, unwilling to release her. He read it over her shoulder. It was a sponsor's pass to the university games at Lake Placid next month. Was she saying she wanted him to go?

"Babe, I was already planning to go to this one. I have my pass…"

"That's not *your* pass." She took a deep breath. "It's mine."

He looked again. Sure enough, her name was printed on it—Jillie Coleman. It was a platinum elite ticket, meaning she'd have access to the private bungalow the sponsors were leasing for patrons to warm up in and enjoy free food and drinks. It also gave her access to a reserve area to watch the races, off to the side of the main grandstands. It would be less crowded, but still compact. He looked from the ticket to her.

"I…I don't mean to sound dense, but…I don't get it."

Her smile was warm, and a little nervous.

"Shane got the pass for me. Mel and I are going to drive up together—it's only three or four hours. Shane has arranged for me to have as much space as possible, and he'll make sure I know the layout of all the sponsor areas. If I can't stay, we'll turn around and come back. I have to at least try." Her smile deepened. "And if I *can* handle it, with some help from my new medication and a few more weeks of therapy, then I thought maybe we could share a room, and Mel and I will drive home the next day. It's not much, but it's a start."

"Let me get this straight…" He kissed her lips softly, speaking low against her skin. "I made arrangements to *stay* in Gallant Lake for you, while you were making arrangements to *leave* Gallant Lake for me?" He kissed her again. "If that's not true love, then I don't know what is."

Chapter Sixteen

Robbie's fingers entwined with Monica's as the sun rose the next morning. It was still a deadly ball of flame and heat. But it didn't frighten Monica any longer. She and Robbie may have to fight again. But not today. And never alone.

Jillie spent a long time kissing Matt. She would have spent even longer if she could, but he finally lifted his head and broke the kiss that had her tingling from head to toe. He was chuckling and shaking his head.

"You and I are a pair, babe. We take a two-week 'break—'" he formed air quotes with his fingers

"—and we both decide to change our lives. Just like that. I'm not a rolling stone, and you are."

"I wouldn't go *that* far, but yes. We're each giving up a part of ourselves that we thought was permanent. Your wanderlust and my…lack of wanderlust."

He lowered his head to whisper in her ear. "I'm liking the sound of all that lust."

Her laughter bubbled up, feeling like a release valve for all the tension of the past few weeks. "I'll bet you do." Her smile faltered. "I missed you, Matt. And it's not just you being gone from Gallant Lake. I missed knowing for sure that you were in my life. It felt like I'd lost an arm or a leg. I'm sorry I didn't answer all those silly, gossipy texts of yours…" He started to protest, but she talked over him. "It took me a while to figure out what I needed to do. I was scared. And when you came back to Gallant Lake but didn't come see me, I'll admit I was hurt. But you kept texting, day after day, and it kept my hope alive. I love you. And if we love each other, that's enough of a foundation for us to build on."

"I agree," Matt said. "I had this idea that love meant the picket fence and minivan life, and I wasn't sure if I could do that. We don't have to have a life that looks like anyone else's, though. We can build our own, you and I."

She nodded. "Shane and Mel figured it out. He travels a lot, but he's never gone for more than a few days at a time. We could handle that, right?"

"We can handle that. We'll find a way. And honestly? Bryce was right when he said he didn't need a chaperone anymore. He's twenty-four. He's going to have to make his own choices. Like you said, my job is done. But if you can figure out a way to come with me once in a while…even if it's Lake Placid or Killington—places we can drive to—that would be great."

"I'm going to try. But if I can't…"

"If you can't, it won't change a thing. I will *never* ask you to do something you're not capable of. I don't ever want to be the cause of pain or stress for you, although I'm sure I will be at times. I'm not perfect by a long shot." He kissed her forehead. "Can I give you a tour of the place? Would that be a good start on going places?"

She was anxious, but not afraid. No one else was there. The layout was open and inviting. She nodded, and he showed her around. Sophie's nails clicked softly on the floor. He was careful to keep to the center of the space, never getting her into a corner. He knew what she needed. A whisper of doubt arrived uninvited. *But would he always?*

They sat on a small sofa near the fireplace, with Sophie at their feet, and he poured brandy into two small glasses. He clinked his glass against hers in a quiet toast, then frowned when he saw her expression.

"What is it?"

She chewed her lip, staring into her glass.

"I'm not *cured*, you know. I'll never really be cured. An anxiety disorder of some form will be with me, and I have no way of knowing how it will manifest itself five years from now." She met his gaze, thankful that he wasn't jumping to tell her everything would be okay. Because they didn't know that. "I'll do my best to manage the agoraphobia. It won't be easy, but I think it's doable. But something else might pop up in my brain. I'll probably always need medication or therapy or both to deal with everyday life. I'll never be…normal."

He waited a moment before answering, his forehead furrowing as if he was searching for words. "Remember when everyone in the world was talking about their lives being the *new normal*? Well, that's what I see our life together as—maybe not normal for someone else, but *our* normal. And that normal will change sometimes. And that's okay. As long as we face it together, Jillie." He lifted her hand and kissed her fingers. "Your anxiety doesn't make you less than perfect. It doesn't make you weak. It does the opposite, babe. It makes you strong. Like… superhero strong." He kissed her lips, cupping one hand behind her head to draw her in. "I'm the goofy sidekick in the story who screws up all the time and eventually gets eaten by the monster."

She laughed, pulling away enough to look into his warm blue eyes, brimming with love for her. "No.

You're the hero in *my* story. The one who inspires me to be stronger than my fears. The one who showed me what love means."

Matt's mouth slanted into an amused smile. "And what *does* it mean?"

"For us? It means security. It means partnership. It means sacrificing a bit of ourselves for the greater good of *us*."

"And hot sex? Can we add that in there somewhere?"

She leaned into his embrace, sliding close enough to straddle him on the sofa.

"I think we can definitely add hot sex. And sweet sex. And all the other types of lovemaking in between."

They kissed, hands sliding up and down each other's body, their actions growing more intense by the second. God, she'd missed him. Missed this. He pulled her onto his lap, and the sofa shook as if manifesting their passion. Except it wasn't passion making it move. It was one large Rottweiler, wanting in on the fun. Sophie sat next to them with her mouth in a wide, sloppy smile. Jillie burst out laughing. Matt groaned and dropped his head to Jillie's shoulder.

"I keep telling you that dog hates me."

"No," she said, patting his hair in sympathy as she giggled. "That dog loves you. Just like I do." Matt lifted his head as she continued. "I love you, and I will love you forever."

He let her kiss him before he answered.

"That's good, because my love is forever, too. I am never letting go of you."

Sophie, apparently satisfied that all was well, curled up next to them, pushing against Matt's leg. He sighed, reaching out to scratch her ears. "Yeah, yeah, I love you too, dog."

Jillie snuggled into his embrace. "We're one big happy family."

He snorted. "I'll agree on the happy part, babe."

Then he kissed her again, and she knew she'd found the one home she'd never want to leave—Matt Danzer's love.

* * * * *

Don't miss out on the rest of the
Gallant Lake Stories miniseries,

A Man You Can Trust
It Started at Christmas
Her Homecoming Wish
Changing His Plans

available now from Harlequin Special Edition!

"We need to get our story straight," she reminded him.

His smile faded. "It's best not to offer too many details.
We met in Atlanta, and now we have Ben."

She turned to face him, adjusting the lap belt as she
shifted. "Your family's not going to question you showing
up with a six-month-old baby? Like maybe you would
have mentioned it to them prior to now?"

One bulky shoulder lifted and lowered. "I told you we
aren't close."

"Your mom not knowing she has a grandchild is a bit
more than 'not close,'" Cory felt compelled to point out.
"Will she be upset we aren't married?"

"I'm not sure."

Her stomach tightened at his response. "Will she want to have a relationship with Ben after this weekend?"

"Good question."

"I have a million of them where that came from," she said. "I don't even know how your father died."

"Heart attack."

"Sudden." She worried her lower lip between her teeth. There were so many potential potholes for her to tumble into this weekend, and based on the tight set of his jaw, Jordan was in no shape to help navigate her through it. In fact, she had the feeling she'd be the one supporting him and he'd need solace well beyond a distraction.

"Can you answer a question with more than two words?" She was careful to make her voice light and was rewarded when his posture gentled somewhat.

"I suppose so."

"A bonus word. Nice. I'm sorry about your father's death," she said, giving in to the urge to reach out and place her hand on his arm.

Don't miss
His Secret Starlight Baby *by Michelle Major,*
available March 2021 wherever
Harlequin Special Edition books and ebooks are sold.

Harlequin.com

Get 4 FREE REWARDS!

We'll send you 2 FREE Books plus 2 FREE Mystery Gifts.

Harlequin Special Edition books relate to finding comfort and strength in the support of loved ones and enjoying the journey no matter what life throws your way.

FREE
Value Over
$20
